CARDS OF LOVE

FIVE OF CUPS

TRISHA WOLFE

'Tis not where we lie, but whence we fell; the loss of heaven's the greatest pain in hell.
 ~Pedro Calderon de la Barca

PROLOGUE

ARCANA KILLER

There's a veil that shrouds our waking world from our nightmares.

This sheer web is a form of protection, a shield. Don't mistake its delicate nature; it's a powerful cloak, as it must be. Should we face the raw truth of ourselves every second of every day, we'd become too impotent, too frail to live.

That is the nightmare, of course. When all our skeletons tumble out, the bones of our past lay bare. Our nightmares exposed to the light.

No one wants their bones picked over. That pain is intolerable.

How many people have we hurt?

Who are our casualties?

It works much like a spider's webbing, ensnaring victims in its sticky trap. A new lover, unaware of the fault line just beneath the veneer, waiting to crack. A tidal wave of self-loathing and shame and guilt to pull us under as we beg to drown, to quiet the storm.

For most, denial is the only coping mechanism. Dress our outsides to contrast what haunts us on the inside.

I smile at this notion as I slip the devil mask over my face.

She shouldn't fear the mask. My veil is her protection.

She's lying on her back as I enter, her eyes closed. She's drowsy from the drug cocktail. I carry her to the corner, where I can prop her against my chest. I shuffle my deck while I breathe in the scent of her shampoo.

Women are so soft, so fragile. This one dresses her outside to denote strength. Independence. Yet I can see the tiny fissure just at her seam, her vulnerability. There's a demon clawing at that crack, trying to break free. Her nightmare slithering like a wisp of smoke into her waking world.

What haunts you?

Her perfect porcelain skin is a tantalizing tease. Silky saccharine. A limerick at play on the tongue. I run the backs of my fingers up her bare arm, unhurriedly, gently, enjoying the way her flesh ripples at my touch.

Her head lolls against my chest as she groans.

"It's time to play," I whisper, my voice a stark command in the pitch-black. I lay the deck before her. "Pick a card."

Everybody has a card.

It's their judgment. Their imminent fate.

The cards don't lie. They offer insight, a choice. If one should fail to accept their path... Well, that's when I appear. If you meet the devil with a Tarot deck...

Run.

Your shadow self has arisen, and seeks retribution.

I'm the reflection of everything vile and wicked that

dwells in your soul, everything you try to keep hidden from the light. I stir the bones.

No one has yet faced their truth and overcome their fate. Every shadow wins, men and women alike choke on the bones. A haunted past too hard to swallow.

The woman in my arms fights the lethargy, unable to lift her hand, so I help her. We turn the card over together.

The Lovers.

"How perfect."

The card depicts a couple in a garden, with a tree and a snake. Like the story of Adam and Eve. Eve was a devious temptress, and Adam suffered because of her deception.

"You must ask yourself," I tell her as I stroke her hair, "are you a woman in love, or are you the snake?"

1

DEVILS AND DETAILS

DR. IAN WEST

Acoustics are important. In a room filled with twelve jurors, one judge, numerous courtroom staff, and a transfixed audience, acoustics are very important. The way someone's voice projects—clear, audible—can make the difference between the defense having to ask the witness to speak up. Repeat themselves. And that witness having time to think and revise their statement.

In a split-second, the witness on the stand blinks and shakes her head lightly. An action delivered so quickly you might miss it, but I see the inferred *no* before she clears her throat and says, "Yes. I'm sure. I was with Quentin Shaver, that man sitting right there—" she points to the man at the defense table "—at the club that night."

I release a sigh. Never mind the head shake, she cleared her throat. A telling clue that the person is about to lie.

I straighten my tie, giving the knot a firm tug. The prosecutor at the table nods once. He got the message.

"Thank you. I have no further questions for this witness, Your Honor." Porter Lovell—God's gift to criminals everywhere—smiles curtly at me before she takes a seat at the defense table with her client.

She should be smiling. Porter has a lot to be happy about right now. If this trial continues to go her way, she'll get Shaver acquitted for murder. A man that was found guilty in the court of public opinion the moment his arrest hit the Internet waves. Beating a murder wrap isn't impossible, but it's damn near for a known criminal once the public chews on it until it's a gnarled, mutilated corpse of a case.

Not to sound insensitive; that's not in relation to the poor deceased woman, who is, in fact, a mutilated corpse.

"Your witness, counselor," Judge Mathers instructs the prosecution.

My client, Assistant District Attorney Eddie Wagner, rises from his chair. With a quick adjustment of his suit, he buttons his jacket and approaches the witness stand. His slicked-back, blond hair gleams in the courtroom lights like the gem he is.

"Here we go," I whisper. Though I've been known to have rambling conversations with myself, I'm actually talking to my assistant. A behavioral analyst I hired when I went rogue with my own trial consultant agency.

"Eddie's got a challenge." Mia's pixie voice comes through my earpiece.

I lift my eyebrows in silent agreement. We started out with ten jurors in our favor—hand-selected through a series of questions during *voir dire*, the jury selection process. It wasn't difficult to establish that many due to Shaver's infamous—*notorious*—media presence.

He's a well-known drug lord.

Ironically enough, Shaver's never been convicted of a

drug crime. Or any crime, for that matter. Because Shaver is also very smart, and because he hires the very best accountants and business people. Drugs are a lucrative smokescreen for his more insidious hobby. Drugs keep the DEA and feds busy looking one way, while he maneuvers the other. Like a magician performing a card trick.

But where are the bodies?

Don't look up his sleeve.

The unfortunate truth is, as long as Shaver pays off the right people, keeping mouths fed and the powerful in power, no one can touch him. Evidence goes missing. Witnesses suddenly disappear.

The prosecution is using the murder charge to make up for the failings of the narcotics unit, going for the maximum sentence: life in prison without parole.

If they can make it stick.

And Porter—the sly minx that she is—has been able to turn four of our jurors in favor of reasonable doubt. We'll get to that later, right now we're focusing on the fact that this time, Shaver made a mistake. He might have been too bold, too cocky. He left a body, with evidence intact on her person. It's so sloppy, I have to wonder if he started using from his own supply.

I sit forward, elbows to knees, as Eddie questions the woman on the witness stand. Jessica Rendell is the defense's star witness. As Shaver's alibi, she places him at a nightclub the evening the victim—Devin Tillman—was murdered in a motel room.

"Ms. Rendell, how often do you frequent The Haze Bar?"

Rendell pushes back in the chair. As is the case with most people testifying in the witness box, they feel apprehensive and on defense when the opposition starts the redirect. They physically distance themselves.

"I'm there just about every weekend," she answers.

Her use of qualifiers gives Eddie an opening to tear her statement apart.

Eddie leans an elbow against the witness stand. He takes her through the events of that Sunday night, as stated by herself and the defendant, lulling her into a rhythm, before he asks, "Are you a magician, Ms. Rendell?"

Defenses lowered, she actually smiles. "Uh, no."

Eddie returns the smile, his megawatt lawyer beam on full display. I love this part.

"Are you sure," he eggs on, "because otherwise, I can't seem to figure out how a person can be in two places at once."

"Objection, Your Honor," Lovell interjects. "Does Mr. Wagner have a question? He's harassing the witness."

"Settle down, counselor. Sustained." Judge Mathers looks at Eddie. "Well, is there a question you'd like to ask this witness?"

"Sorry, Your Honor. Yes, there is." Eddie goes to the prosecution table and gathers a file. As he walks slowly, deliberately toward the witness stand, he flips through the pages within. "Ms. Rendell, at approximately eleven forty-five on the night in question, your phone's GPS logged you at a residence in Bristol Heights."

She scratches her arm, eyes darting around the room. A clear sign that the mention of the trap house—*drug* house— where she gets her fix is making her fiend. That's how she came to be a witness for Shaver, of course. A paid witness. Promised an endless supply of her drug of choice.

I glance at Porter. On cue, she stands. "Objection. Not in

evidence, Your Honor. Where did Mr. Wagner obtain this information?"

Exasperated, the judge looks toward Eddie, eyebrows raised.

Eddie clears his throat. "I was just made aware of this discovery myself, Your Honor. This morning. But it proves the alibi Ms. Rendell is providing for Mr. Shaver is false, and therefore—"

"You'll provide the defense with this discovery," Judge Mathers interrupts, "and give the defense until the afternoon to conduct their own investigation."

Porter Lovell is not happy. "Your Honor, that's not much time to investigate—"

"Will tomorrow morning be sufficient for the defense?" the judge asks, an edge in his tone. Though he has to remain unbiased, even he's having a difficult time not looking at Shaver with disdain.

From my viewpoint, Porter doesn't appear pleased, her lips pursed into that tight little frown of hers. But she knows better than to argue with Mathers. "Yes, Your Honor. Thank you."

The judge adjourns the trial for the day, and the courtroom rises to stand.

Eddie looks at me expectantly. His question clear: *Do we have him?*

I give a half-nod, half-shrug that confuses the ADA. "Thanks" he mouths.

Knowing what someone *wants* to do is different than knowing what they'll actually do. In the case of a jury, once they're behind closed doors to deliberate, I'm just as anxious as a defendant in the hot seat.

It's exhilarating.

The secret phone that Rendell had under her ex-husband's account can help Eddie's case, since I'm 99% sure that Shaver and his crew didn't know about it. Rendell wants her lifetime fix more than she cares about the jeopardy she's put her life in by lying to Shaver.

And that's the kind of alliance you get with addicts. The only way Shaver was going to be brought down was if he made a mistake. Well, in my professional opinion, he just made a big one by putting his fate in Rendell's hands.

Now, to get the DNA thrown out.

Thrown out, you say? I know. Usually, DNA in a murder case means a slam-dunk. It's the nail in the coffin. The indisputable fact. And because of this, criminals have found ways to use DNA to their advantage, rather than against them.

In this case, Shaver's semen was presented on Rendell's skirt. She claims they were intimately together at The Haze Club, so therefore he couldn't have been with Tillman, murdering and mutilating her at a motel.

Juries love DNA. They used to not know what the hell it was. Now they believe in it like it's gospel. The trick is in convincing them that DNA can be inconclusive. That depending on who does the testing, it can be contaminated, planted. After years of training people to trust in the science, we're now trying to undo just that.

It's a tricky catch twenty-two, since we're also asking them to believe the DNA found at the crime scene.

Which is damn difficult, being that motel rooms are a nest of DNA from hundreds, if not thousands, of people. Porter's prospect to get our DNA discovery thrown out bodes much more in her favor.

And then there's the little annoying fact of motive. To prove Shaver committed this heinous murder, we have to prove intent. It's not enough to disprove his alibi, or even corroborate he was with Tillman. That's all arguable without a clear motive.

And for Shaver, a man I've had the pure displeasure of analyzing throughout this trial, I can attest he's a natural born psychopath with antisocial personality disorder—which means the only motive he needs is the desire in his black little heart.

Making him the hardest to pin a motive on.

As Eddie packs his briefcase, I look at the jury. How are they taking Rendell's testimony? Do they believe it? Do they trust her?

Trial science isn't an exact science. It's social science. A healthy scoop of psychology with a dash of sociology. Mix and bake, and the end result is a cake with as little bias in the jury pool as possible.

It's fucking harder than you think.

As a society, every last one of us harbors bias against something.

But that's where I come in to even the playing field. Reading facial cues—microexpressions—and discerning their biases in order to develop a jury of twelve individuals that will give my clients the fairest trial possible.

It's also helpful to do a little tech digging and accessing the jurors' social media accounts, to find out how often they're online. What they like. What they comment on. There's a wealth of knowledge on social media. And we use it.

I get to know each juror personably, intimately. We become lovers during a trial.

Well, that's taking it a bit far. We're more like besties. I learn what makes them tick, their tells, and how to apply that during a trial. If you want to convince someone—twelve someones—that a murder happened a certain way, you have to build a narrative they'll believe. One that weaves a conceivable story they're able to follow.

Our golden rule: Keep it simple stupid.

That's how we erase any doubt. What the defense is hinging their acquittal on.

If you believe the narrative, if you think you're smarter than the man trying to dupe the system, then bam. We got you.

Everyone believes they're smarter than the average person.

All the prosecution has to do is lead the jury to the fountain of knowledge. Let them drink the Kool-Aid. Or whatever mixed, fucked-up metaphor you want to apply here. The point is, we might be tenacious in how we get a conviction, but it's for the greater good.

At least, that's how I'm able to sleep peacefully at night.

That, and a wave simulator machine that mimics the ocean.

It's very soothing.

After the judge releases the jury, I take mental snapshots of each one as they file out. The game is tied six to six.

As I ease out of the pew, Porter turns my way and winks.

Sly minx. "Game on," I whisper.

"What's that?" Mia asks in my ear.

"Nothing." I straighten my tie and adjust the mic transmitter.

"Eddie handled the cross well," Mia says.

"Agreed," I say, nodding to a gray-haired woman who is giving me the stink-eye because it appears I'm talking to myself. I head out of the courtroom. "Now all I need from you is the good news."

Mia's chiming laugh tickles my ear. "What about the bad news? You don't want that first?"

I blow out a heavy breath. "Please be fucking with me. There is no bad news, right?"

Eddie meets me in the corridor across from the bathrooms. "Mia?"

I nod. "Great job in there."

"Thanks, boss."

Technically, he's my boss. But ever since he first walked into my six-floor office, a beaten down, newly appointed ADA, and I told him exactly how it was going to be (my way or the…you get it), and we won our first case, he accepted the hierarchy. The pecking order, if you will.

It's semantics, anyway.

I press my finger to my earpiece so I can hear Mia more clearly. "What did you say?"

"I said, I got some information on juror number two. Her husband was injured on site today and was rushed to the ER. She might be pulled."

"Dammit." I say this a little too loudly, and the same woman from inside the courtroom passes by with a raised, gray eyebrow.

"Sorry, ma'am." I give her my panty-melting smile.

She shakes her head and keeps going, clutching her cardigan closed tightly at the neck.

Eh, I'm an acquired taste.

"She's one of ours," I say, not as loudly this time. "I know she is. I can read it in her eyes every time she looks at Shaver. She wants to nail his dick to the floor."

Eddie matches my pace once we're outside. We head down the courthouse steps. "Drinks?" he asks.

"Not tonight. I got a thing."

He nods knowingly. "Ah, *that* thing. See you in the morning, then." He crosses the street toward his BMW. You might think that's a little flashy for an ADA, and you'd be right. Eddie's family is affluent; he doesn't have to work in government. So the fact that he trudges through the underbelly of the justice system every day, fighting the good fight, speaks to his character, and why I like him.

Also, he's the one lawyer in the DA's office that can afford my retainer.

He throws his briefcase in the backseat and leaves me at the steps, wondering why I didn't just go with him. I could use a drink before...

"I'm disconnecting now, Mia. I'll talk to you in the morning."

A weighty beat. Then: "Say hi to Melanie for me, Dr. West."

Thankfully, the line clicks dead before she can hear the raw noise that works its way free. Like shoving a hot poker down my throat. The burning ache is always there, amplified every time someone says her name.

2

THE GIFT

DR. IAN WEST

A nice dose of numb is what I need right about now.

I pull my flask from the inseam of my blazer and twist off the silver cap. Swallow two long gulps. The evening air is tinged with smoke and dead leaves; the scent of fall in the city, where chimneys billow puffs of gray into the air, clearing out months of nonuse.

That scent—the first hint of winter—used to put me at ease. Quiet my ever-present thrum of stress. I work in a high anxiety kind of atmosphere, where every case brings a certain level of demand. And when we'd walk down the sidewalk and get that first whiff of fall, Melanie would say: "Time for the lion to slumber."

Now, as I smell the smoke drifting through the crisp air, dread takes up residency within me, a reminder of that phone call three years ago. It's like waiting for a bomb to go off. But it never does. There's just the trepidation, the apprehension. The wait for something bad to happen.

I empty my flask and mutter a curse. Not nearly enough. My destination is five blocks away. I'm so close, but a pit stop won't take long. Luckily, The Bar is just one block to my right.

I make the detour and, as I enter the bar, it's already lively with the after work crowd. Young executives and of course lawyers, being that it's in the downtown Courthouse District. No one wants to roam too far to find a watering hole.

I lean my elbows on the bar top and order a shot of bourbon. "Make that two," I amend to the bartender. What? Might as well be realistic. My clients lie for a living. I don't.

"Can you make that three? Put it on his tab."

My eyes close at the sound of her voice. "Porter Lovell. No escaping you today, is there?"

I can feel her body heat along my left side. I have the urge to slide closer, knock her off the stool. But that would be a little too crass, I think. Even for me.

Her deep breath sounds as irritated as she always appears lately. "If you want to avoid lawyers, West, you should probably avoid bars. Especially The Bar."

"What's up with that name, anyway? Is it some kind of play on passing the bar? Or a reference to Gone Girl? All you defense attorneys love that book, right? Crazy Amy got away with murder. She must be your hero."

Her smirk makes the cute dimple in her cheek pop. I look away, resenting that dimple. It's hard to portray an incensed, scorned adversary when your opponent is so damn beautiful. The world is mocking that way.

Porter hooks her dark waves behind her ear. "And who's your hero, West?"

The bartender sets the shots in front of me. I give him a curt nod before tipping one back. I breathe out a sharp breath from the burn. "I prefer having no hero, Porter. Makes it harder to be disappointed in people when they fail."

"And people always fail you, don't they?"

"Nah ah." I waggle a finger at her. "Leave reading people to the professionals. But speaking of work—"

"I am not discussing the case with you." She takes down half her shot.

I smile, mainly to myself. Once upon a time, Porter was a prosecutor. A damn good one. Oh, the righteous convictions of youth. How we believe early on that we're going to change the world, right the wrongs, and all that bullshit.

Then reality sets in. Which usually happens right around the time the importance of money makes itself known. At least, I think that was the case with Porter. She used to drive a Honda. Now she rolls up to court in a Bentley GT. She's made a hell of a name for herself these past few years.

Anyway, Mel and Porter started off in the same firm. Two prosecuting lawyers taking on the system. Melanie was the reason I got involved in all this legal crap to begin with. I wasn't a young idealist. Yeah, *hardly*. I just didn't want my hard-earned psychology degree to go to waste, which it seamed to be doing at an expedited rate with the economy. My future was looking bleak, with the choice to work within general counseling (shoot me now; I fucking hate whiny married couples), or waiting tables.

Honestly, I made a killing at F&B (that's food and beverage for the ones who never had to flip burgers during college).

Then Melanie invited me into an interview with one of her clients. She wanted me to get a read on him, to discover if he was lying.

Because, even though Mel was a prosecutor, she didn't

just take on any case. She had to believe in their virtue, in their pursuit to sue, in the truth of their testimony.

Being on the right side was important to Mel. She was an angel in a sea of devils. If she took a case, it was because she cared. It became not just a case but a cause. And she'd work herself to death fighting for it.

I stare down at the amber liquid in the tiny glass.

When Melanie died, she took with her the best of all of us. Including Porter.

"She'd understand…" Porter starts. "It's my job, West. I took an oath to represent my client zealously and to the best of my ability. I don't have to like him—"

"I was wrong, Porter. You do read people pretty well." I dig out a couple of bills from my wallet and drop them on the counter, where I leave my second shot of bourbon. Then I look her right in her golden eyes. "Enjoy the drinks," I say, when what I really want to voice is just how disappointed Mel would be in her for representing Shaver.

Mel was the nonjudgmental angel. Not me. Judging people is what I do best.

"Wait, West…"

There's something in her voice that makes my insides quiver. *Anguish.* That's what it is, and I have the sudden impulse to comfort her. Make her pain stop. Dammit. The bourbon in my stomach burns, the ache in my chest hard to breathe around. I need to get far away. Right now.

"I'm late for a thing, Lovell. See you tomorrow."

"I hate when you call me that."

I make it to the door, almost free, but her voice chases after me, far too close. "She was my friend, too. I miss Melanie…especially today—"

I push the door open, thankful for the brisk rush of air that hits my fiery skin, and the city noise that drowns out her voice. I can't fall victim to Porter, to the past. Not today.

I hit the sidewalk with heavy steps, moving fast and far away from Porter and her memories and her sympathetic tone. It's a noxious mix that won't change anything; only makes my anger spike. And I try really hard not to be *that* guy.

Rounding the street corner, I spot the cemetery sign. I only come here once a year. And I come here alone. On the first anniversary of Melanie's death, Eddie, Mia, Porter and every other person in the greater DC area, made the attempt to be here. Sort of a group effort, a show of support. It felt more like an intervention, and I quickly remedied that.

I didn't show.

Later, when each approached me in turn, I claimed I'd forgotten the date. They saw through my bullshit, of course, but it was established—in my preferred unsaid way; very passive-aggressive, I admit—that I wanted this day to myself.

I'll work. I'll go about my day like any other. But at 7:00 p.m. on the first of October, the hour of the phone call, the hour that Melanie was taken from this fucked up world—that hour belongs to me.

I don't share my grief.

Actually, I'm a hoarder of grief.

I pile it up into a tight little ball every year and stuff it into a dark corner. I think it's located beneath my left rib cage. I've amassed a nice collection of decaying grief balls over the past few years. That's probably where the extra pounds came from.

The gate to the cemetery is open, and I walk in like an expected guest.

Melanie's grave is located in her family plot. Her

mother's side of the family has lived in the city since the turn of the century (last century; not this one. I'm showing my age). We had planned to purchase—very expensively—my own plot for our bones to lay, side-by-side, lovers in the afterlife. But then the unthinkable happened.

It's always the *unthinkable*. Because really, who the hell thinks about their fiancé getting hit by a car while walking home to their second-floor loft? Just two blocks away. She was one minute from being with me…and then she was gone. A hit and run.

The bastard who murdered the love of my life was never found.

According to the ER doctor, it happened instantaneously. By the time Melanie arrived via ambulance to the hospital, she was already pronounced dead. He said this to me as if it would bring some form of comfort.

She died instantaneously.

I punched him.

I was removed from the hospital very promptly after that. I never got to see her in that cold, stale place, and maybe, in some way, that's for the best. The sight of Melanie's lifeless body isn't one of my memories of her.

Her mother opted for a closed casket. She couldn't bear to see Mel in that state either—she was gone. Gone. Just gone. The funeral just a ceremony based on etiquette because that's what people do.

As I head farther in, I stuff my hands in my jacket pockets. I finger the charm there, the anniversary gift I bring her every year. It might be kind of morbid to celebrate a death anniversary, but as I'm a psychologist, it's my own coping mechanism. Our wedding was to be a few weeks later. Mel loved Halloween. We were getting married on All

Hallows' Eve. She was a bit twisted like that. I smile at the thought.

So I know she'd love the little silver witch charm.

The white marble headstone is up ahead, and my chest pangs with that familiar ache. The closer I get, the more real the pain. I do a decent job of distancing myself from it most of the time. Sarcasm helps. No one can get close to a sarcastic asshole.

But seeing the headstone, knowing her body is just six feet below...

I stop before the white marble and breathe. I drag a deep breath into my lungs to expand the aching pressure trying to squeeze the life out of me.

I know some people like to talk to their dead loved ones. Talk to the headstone like it's just been sitting there, resting, waiting like some ethereal entity for dumb fuckers to unload their burdens.

I can't talk to her.

I dig out the silver witch and set it on the base of the marble. Melanie and I...well, I don't have to say anything. I never had to voice myself when she was alive. She could read me with one look. At times, I hated and loved that about her. There was no hiding my emotions from her.

So being here, it's like opening a vein.

All that piled up grief bursts through the dam, cracking my rib cage as it flows.

I will always be the man who loves Melanie Harper.

I don't have to tell her I miss her every fucking second of the day. I don't have to say what a shit I've turned into without her. Or that this life is bitter now that she's gone.

She knows all of this, because wherever she is, she can see right through me.

When I've had my fill of the pain, I turn to go, but something catches my eye.

I kneel down on the dry earth of dead grass and leaves and swipe my hand across the grave. Someone else has left her a gift. Tucked beneath the leaves is a card. A black-and-white design on the back…and as I flip it over, an image of a cloaked man and cups.

I frown, eyes squinted. What the hell? It's old. Tinged with age and use.

A Tarot card.

A surge of electric apprehension hits my chest, ice-cold as it webs through my veins. Months of research come at me fast, my mind finding the threads and linking them together. This isn't a gift.

It's a warning.

A threat.

From Shaver.

3

MY CUP RUNNETH OVER

DR. IAN WEST

Come the next morning, the city is still asleep, nestled in a womb of dark comfort. The sounds that normally thrum and pulse with the beat of the capital are vacant from my office window.

I chug my coffee and then open my laptop. Eddie beats my small staff through the door this morning. He looks sleep rumpled, regardless of his pressed suit and gelled hair.

He tosses his briefcase on my desk with feigned annoyance. "So what's up, doc? Shaver hang himself in the cell last night?"

I set my cup down. "Is that the way you want to win the case?"

"Too early for psychoanalysis," he mutters.

"I hate when people get those mixed up." I brace my palms on the desk. "Freud is psychoanalysis. I'm not asking about your wet dreams that may or may not center around your mother."

"That's fucked up, doc."

"It's simply *analyze*. It's too early for analyzing you, which I agree. And no, Shaver didn't hang himself. The trial is still on for today. Just waiting on Mia and Charlie to get here."

He studies me a bit too intently. "Yesterday went okay?"

I cast my gaze down at the files on my desk. Give them a quick shuffle. "That's what we're meeting about." As Mia and Charlie walk in, I nod briefly in acknowledgement, then dive in. "Yesterday evening, I found this in the cemetery."

I pull out the Tarot card that I placed in a baggie and hold it up so they can get a look at both sides.

Mia, wearing her signature all-black to match her dyed-black hair, cranes an eyebrow. "The Five of Cups?"

Of course she'd know. Mia is a master of all trades. If she researches something once, she can recall if forever. Not eidetic memory, just a damn good one.

"The Five of Cups," I confirm, "from the Minor Arcana. It was placed on Melanie's grave."

Eddie shakes his head. "Shaver?"

Charlie, my investigator, pipes in. "Shaver has an affinity for the Tarot. It's how he selects his victims. Allegedly."

Mia sets her oversized bag on her chair. "It's in one of the interview transcripts. From…" She snaps her fingers until it comes to her. "From his crony, Lyle Fisher. Charlie and I were working on him to testify, but he backed out. Witness protection wasn't very appealing."

This bit of information settles over the team in silent understanding. Then Eddie looks at me. "Shaver is trying to scare us off."

I ding an imaginary bell. "Me, actually. I think the card was meant to imply that I'm now in his crosshairs."

Eddie furrows his brow. "How do you know it's directed toward you?"

"Grief," Mia says, and glances at the card. "The Five of Cups denotes loss and sorrow."

Another uncomfortable silence follows, and I clear my throat. "It can be interpreted a few different ways," I say, pulling up my research on the laptop. "But yeah, Mia's big brain is right. If I were a Tarot card, I'd be the sullen guy in a cloak, staring at the overturned cups."

"Your back to the full ones," Mia adds. "Looking at what was lost, instead of what you still have."

"Christ, Mia. Downer much?" I try to lighten the mood.

She shrugs unapologetically. "I call it like I see it, Dr. West."

I pocket the card in my suit jacket inseam.

"Are we taking it to the police?" Charlie asks.

Always my do-gooder. Charlie was raised by a cop, and he's still at that young, idealistic age in his twenties where things appear black and white. Good and bad. Right and wrong. Blah blah.

"Not going to the cops, and not telling Lovell, either." I cross my arms. "If Shaver is trying to make me back off from helping the prosecution, that means we're hitting a nerve on the case. We're closing in on Rendell today, exposing her testimony. With no alibi, Eddie can turn up the heat on the motel DNA. And I want you to do just that."

Mia's pixie features purse in uncertainty. "I'm a skeptic, but I'm not so skeptical when people take the power to control fate in their own hands."

I shake my head, exasperated. "What does that mean?"

She fists her hands on her petite hips. "The Tarot, Dr.

West. People believe in it, and that belief gives it power. I think you should play this one a bit more cautiously."

I sigh out a long breath. "Duly noted, Mia dear. Now, can we all get back on the reality train before court? I think we can use this to stir the defense."

We set up the big screen with the mirrored projection of my laptop, and I go over—or rather, I have Mia go over—the cards and their meanings. I have no idea if Quentin Shaver really believes in this shit or not, but I want him to know I got the message.

And I'm not backing down.

The truth of the matter is, he had one of his twisted little cronies put that card on Melanie's grave. His filth violated her sacred place, where the love of my life rests.

That pisses me off.

When I get pissed, I tend to take it out on people. The bad guys. I put all my effort into taking them down, and Shaver just messed with the wrong trial consultant.

Before the trial commences, Porter does a fine job of ignoring me in the courtroom. I've tried to catch her eye, to offer her my charming smile, but she keeps her focus glued to her phone until Shaver is brought in and seated next to her.

Admittedly, I feel a little guilty for how I left things between us.

Also, I doubt she knows what her client is up to. I really want to believe that, if she had any idea he had that card delivered to Mel's gravesite, she'd be just as upset. Shaver's making it personal. It's time to put this case to bed. For all of us.

The bailiff leads in the jury, and sure as shit, juror number two has been replaced with an alternate. Dammit. One of ours down.

"Mia, get the profile up on the board for the first alternate."

"Already on it," she says.

We're asked to stand as Judge Mathers is announced.

Porter looks back at me. It's just a second, a glimpse, but I see the desperation in her creased eyes. The apology is there; she knows I can read this from her. Maybe she regrets taking the case. Maybe she knows what Shaver has done, or is attempting to do by trying to intimidate me. And maybe she knows it won't work, that Shaver has ended any chance he had at winning his freedom. Thereby taking her career down a big peg.

Or maybe I want to see all that there—to believe in who she once was before our lives were torn apart.

What can I say? I'm a romantic at heart. Or I was once.

Shaver glances at me before he takes a seat. I've looked at him plenty during the course of this trial. I've studied his features, his expressions. His body language. I've witnessed what the jury fails to see when he gives them his sincere, practiced smiles and sad little puppy dog eyes. I know what lurks beneath.

The devil.

Not in the Biblical sense. More of a metaphorical evil. The absence of morality, of conscience. Most people work hard to control their features in order to hide their emotions. Shaver is the opposite. He works hard to display emotions. To convince others he *feels*.

Yet there's a void, an absence of substance, where his soul

should be. Or whatever you want to call it. The thing that gives us depth. That awareness.

He's only aware of what he wants and how to obtain it.

It's the selfish part of the mind that is supposed to mature with age. In psychopaths, this part of the psyche is stunted and never fully develops. The id—the part that demands immediate gratification—is in constant need, requiring a fix. More more *more*.

That's my professional analysis, anyway. At least from what I've deduced sitting five rows away from him for the past week. I could dig deeper, get him in a room with just the two of us, but honestly, I'm a little terrified of what that shell of a human might entice me to do to him.

A crooked smile curves his lips as he stares at me, then Porter touches his shoulder, silently motioning him to face the front.

I cement my expression, schooling my features in a cool, neutral countenance that says, *hey buddy, I don't rattle*. But that touch...

For the briefest moment, when Porter laid her hand on him, all the air in my lungs evaporated. A crushing collapse of my chest cavity. And I felt my features fall. A microexpression slipped through—one that I'm not sure Shaver caught.

Disgust. Hurt. Envy.

We never just feel one emotion; it's a twisted mesh. That's why it's so difficult for people to express verbally what they're feeling when a therapist asks just that. *How do you feel?* I know this—and yet I'm still baffled by my reaction.

Examining my twisted mesh of feelings for Porter will take more time than I have right now, so instead I give my attention to the court. Rendell is being reminded of her swear-in. When she's seated in the witness box, the judge asks Porter if the defense has had sufficient time to investigate the phone records.

Porter stands. "We have, Your Honor. Thank you."

My eyebrows hike in surprise. Although there was nothing much to investigate, as the records were straightforward, I'm still shocked by Porter's lack of fight. She should at least try to have them removed from evidence.

And when someone surprises me…

I cover my mouth to muffle my voice. "Mia, what don't we know about the GPS?"

"Nothing. Why?"

One of those annoying feelings—like you forgot to turn off the oven—stirs in my subconscious, as if we overlooked a piece of the puzzle.

"I don't know," I whisper to Mia. "Just…you and Charlie do another search. Look at every angle. Find out what we missed."

"I'm not sure where—"

"Look at everything again," I snap.

The man in the row ahead glances back and shushes me.

Mia's quiet for a long beat. Then: "I'll see what I can find."

I set my apprehension on the back burner (another oven reference; not good), and tune in to Eddie's cross of Rendell.

She looks more poised today, more put together. Prepared. Porter's done a good job of prepping her.

Eddie gives her his megawatt lawyer smile. "Morning, Ms. Rendell." He asks a few warm-up questions to get going, inquiring about her evening, and to most this seems like a pointless practice in etiquette, but Eddie's brain is a sponge.

One slip on her part later, one thing that doesn't line up with any of her testimony, and he'll be on it like a dog with a bone.

"Now, where were we." Eddie braces his hands on the witness stand. "Your phone and where your location was tracked through the GPS. Do you have a phone, Ms. Rendell?"

"Yes, I do."

Eddie nods. "And who set this service up for you?"

"My ex-husband."

Her answers are clipped and straightforward. Not good.

Getting the same read on the witness, Eddie switches it up to get a more emotional reaction. "You and your ex-husband get along, do you?"

Rendell's forehead creases. "Most of the time."

He nods repeatedly. "Because, I mean, I have an ex myself. Props to you and yours for handling the divide of assets and money with class."

She shrugs. "We try. But you see, the phone he set up wasn't for me."

"Oh really?"

"My ex-husband set it up for our daughter."

Mother. Fuck.

I look at Porter. She's just sitting there. Cool as an ice queen. No reaction to her very obvious victory. Shaver is also stoic. Two peas in a fucking pod.

Mia's voice crackles in. "Shit."

Yeah. Shit. As in this case just turned into a big pile of it.

"Get verification that the phone was with the daughter," I tell Mia. "Quickly."

"On it."

We did our research, and we did it well—but it's hard to combat a lie with: *nah uh*. You need evidence. Because it's a believable lie. Father buys daughter phone and sets up her account to keep in touch with her. I look at the jury, and yup, they're buying it.

Eddie glances at me, and I tap my ear, letting him know I have Mia on it. He drags the redirect out. "How old is your daughter?"

"Seventeen."

"That's a fun age," Eddie says. "Is she in school?"

"Yes."

"What grade?"

"Senior."

Eddie looks at me again. I shake my head. No update yet.

He clears his throat. "So, Ms. Rendell, you expect us to believe that—" he glances at the jury, making sure they're included "—your daughter, who is in high school, was out at a known drug house at nearly midnight on a school night?"

Eddie's good, on the right track. The father buying the daughter a phone is believable, even makes the parents look decent, like concerned parents keeping tabs on their child. It's new information to the jury that the location is a trap house, and the appall is scribbled on their faces.

Rendell—regardless of her addiction—is still human. As such, her shame is real. Actually, drug addicts carry more shame than the average person because of who they are, and Eddie's forcing her to war with her self-preservation over being seen as a loving mother versus her need for the drug.

Who was at the trap house getting a fix? Mother or daughter?

When Porter prepped her, Rendell probably made a bargain with herself in order to sellout her daughter on the witness stand. *Just this last time.* It's the addicts' credo.

Rendell swallows hard, her throat dipping with her internal struggle. "I don't know…"

"So who was at that house, Ms. Rendell? You or your daughter?"

Porter stands. "Objection, Your Honor. Asked and answered. The witness has already answered Mr. Wagner's question once."

Judge Mathers appears unsure. "I'll allow it. I'm curious myself to hear the witness's knowledge of this situation."

Score one point for the good guys.

Rendell scratches her arm. "My daughter was. It's her phone."

Oh, how low we sink.

Disgust resonates throughout the jury. But it's not enough. They may dislike her, but that doesn't change the fact of the case for Shaver. We still have to prove Rendell wasn't with Shaver to kill his alibi.

The new juror is a bit of a question mark. I focus on her, trying to get a read. She's in her late forties. Short blond hair. Manicured without being overly dressy. She just seems… average. Which I hate. Average people are the hardest to read.

Mia comes through. "I need more time to find out where the daughter was that night."

I give Eddie a clipped head shake and quickly swipe my finger across my neck. We have nothing. End it.

Eddie turns toward the judge. "I reserve the right to question this witness at a later time, Your Honor."

Judge Mathers nods, although he looks surprised by Eddie's choice to postpone questioning. "You may, counselor. Do you have a witness to call to the stand?"

Eddie straightens his suit, stands taller. "No, Your Honor."

Because we haven't worked Lyle Fisher hard enough to turn on Shaver. And because we haven't decided whether or not to call Shaver to the stand. If we can't prove Rendell was at the trap house to discredit his alibi...then calling the defendant might be our only way to expose his nature.

You can't get a conviction by proving someone's a psychopath.

But you can turn enough jurors against said psychopath.

The way we plan to do that—if it comes down to the last stand—is the Tarot card.

If Shaver was so bold to send me one, then it's possible it's part of his MO. While we're in court, I have Charlie combing the past two years' worth of homicides that include this MO and Shaver's kill method as parameters. Charlie is seeking any mention of the Arcana or Tarot in connection to homicide cases.

It might be a stretch, as I'm not Shaver's ideal victim. The card could only be meant as a threat. But men like Shaver —*scratch that*—monsters like Shaver have very specific routines. They're methodical. They enjoy the hunt just as much as the kill.

And he's limited as to who he can hunt behind bars.

Using a proxy to do his bidding may muffle the pleasure he gleans from the hunt and the kill, but he'd still experience the anticipation. The rush. The climax through his surrogate.

Anyway, as I was saying, a serial killer has a routine, a ritual. This ritual gives them immense pleasure. If reading the Tarot is part of Shaver's victim selection process, then there's evidence somewhere out there to prove this.

Mia and Charlie just need to unearth it in time.

The judge calls a recess for lunch, and I walk up the isle

to meet Eddie. "Mia's working on getting proof of where the daughter actually was that night," I whisper to him.

He nods knowingly. "Rendell is a waste of space. The jury senses that. We need that DNA thrown out, that's what we need."

Shaver's little swimmers on Rendell's skirt. Which, technically, could've ended up there at any point during that night, either before or after Tillman was murdered. But again: proof.

Without proof, we're just kids kicking dirt at each other in a sandbox.

So, the best plan of attack is to have that sample thrown out altogether. Then once we discredit Shaver's alibi, it makes it easier for the prosecution to put Shaver in the motel room with Tillman.

I.e. Shaver's DNA presented by the prosecution.

That's the ideal way the trial will go.

Let's look at it from a not so good angle.

In a case like this where there's conflicting DNA, where one sample proves innocence and the other guilt, only one can survive. DNA Thunderdome. Two DNA enter, one DNA leaves.

I amuse myself.

Right. So two men. That's what the jury will hear when the prosecution brings in the motel DNA. That the victim was intimate with two men that night, and that one of them was Shaver. But because the lab where the DNA was tested butchered the only sample, there's no way to retest it for a second analysis.

Which means Porter has a good chance of getting our sample tossed.

Touché.

But if she can't, then her plan of attack will most likely cause her to sink pretty low, citing the victim was the type of woman who slept with two men at once. Victim blaming and shaming can backfire with a jury in a political sense, but condemning the victim for her sex life won't matter to Porter. It won't affect the case she's building. It's what she needs to muddy the water with doubt. Quite literally, muddy the evidence enough that the jury can't convict.

For Porter to get the motel DNA thrown out, she has to prove the sample was corrupted either before or during testing. We have an expert witness all lined up for DNA analysis to counter this.

Other than the sample discovered on Tillman's person, we have Shaver's fingerprints found on the motel bathroom counter. Shaver was there, in that room, but so were about 600 other people leaving behind their fingerprints and DNA samples.

Hotel/motel room crime scenes are an evidence cluster fuck.

My chest just tightened.

I rub the achy air bubble between my rib cage, and Eddie eyes me suspiciously. "Everything okay, doc?"

"It will be as soon as we get Dominic on the stand," I assure him. Dominic is our expert in the field of DNA.

Eddie sighs. "I'm sure Lovell will have a follow up witness even for him. Man, she's getting tough to beat. I miss the old days, when she was on my side."

Yeah. I look over at Porter, and she's staring right back at me. She ticks her head in a manner that means she wants to talk. My chest flutters with a curious prickly feeling. Elation? I tamp it down.

"I'll check in with you before the next session," I tell him, then make my way toward Porter.

Shaver is being shackled to be taken to the holding cell, and right before the court officer takes him away, he leans in to Porter and whispers in her ear. I stop. The sight a punch to the gut.

His gaze roves up to find me, his lips curling into that snide smile.

After he's led away, I approach Porter. "Ready to offer a plea deal already?" I am sarcasm's ugly cousin. Which I guess would be pessimism? This case is wearing on me.

The serious burn of her eyes makes me drop my contemptuous smile. "I'll trade you my DNA sample if you trade me yours? Oh wait." She holds up a finger in mock point-making fashion. "Yours was all used up, leaving me no way to test it. Convenient."

I shrug. "Or maybe not so."

She sighs. "Actually, yes. I want to talk to you about a deal."

I shake my head. "I don't get it. What's the catch?"

She tucks a stray hair behind her ear. "My client wants to talk to you. Alone."

4

MIND GAMES

DR. IAN WEST

The courthouse conference room is stark white and bare. Ironically (that word has lost all meaning), back in college, I learned that bare walls were best when it comes to counseling disturbed minds.

Fitting, that I'm about to speak with Shaver for the first time in this room, where there's nothing to distract us from one another.

The jangle of chains interrupts the silence before the door opens. The guard escorts Shaver inside and seats him in the chair adjacent from me. Porter follows suit and takes up his other side. The officer lingers in the corner.

Tension thickens the air-conditioned room as we wait for one of us to begin. Porter pulls out a file and opens it on the table.

I lean back in my chair, the squeak too loud in the still room. "This is like a game of don't blink without the eye contact. Kind of awkward."

Porter exhales audibly. "Dr. West, if this is a waste of my client's time—"

"No." I hold up my hands in surrender. "I'm intrigued. Applicably, you'd strike a bargain with the ADA, not the consultant." I look at Shaver while addressing this. He's steadily watching me. "So I'm curious what you think I can do for you, Mr. Shaver."

Shaver's intense gaze doesn't waver as he says to Porter, "I need to be alone with the good doctor."

She shakes her head. "I strongly advise against that."

"We're in good hands." I nod to the guard. "We have an officer to keep us rowdy boys in line."

Porter glances at me and then looks to Shaver. She blows out a terse breath. "This is so unorthodox." But she collects her file and briefcase and stands. "I'll be right outside the room. Fifteen minutes. That's how much time you have."

I tilt my head as I watch her exit the room. She's edgy, more so than usual. She has a lot riding on the outcome of this case, but it's more than career oriented, her concern. Something has her shaken.

"You got her pretty worked up," I say to Shaver.

He eases back in the metal chair. "Oh, I can't take all the credit, Dr. West. You and Ms. Lovell have history, don't you?"

We're not going there. "What is it that you want?"

"A diagnosis."

My smile is forced. "In fifteen minutes? I'm flattered you hold such faith in my abilities. But that's not possible."

He chuckles. His voice is a smooth baritone. I imagine it's one of his assets when it comes to luring women into his web. The British accent isn't a bad touch, either.

"I'll agree to change my plea. Innocent by reason of

insanity," he clarifies. "And you'll agree to be my psychologist."

"And the laughs don't stop there, folks."

"I'm serious."

"Oh, I know you are. That's what makes this so entertaining." I sit forward and lace my hands together on the table. "You can't change your plea in the middle of a trial. Judges tend to frown on that. Big time."

He adjusts the collar of his pressed, white shirt. "Porter can make it happen."

A sick feeling churns in my gut at his informal use of her name. "I'll agree to an evaluation and expert testimony," I say, sitting back. I hate breathing the same air as him. "And you'll agree to ask for a new trial and new representation."

A one-shot deal. I don't want to spend months or possibly even *years* as this deviant's psychologist. But I do want Porter away from him. Far, far away.

Shaver studies me closely. I'm showing my hand, my weakness. But he's intelligent enough to have figured that out. Any bluff I might have concerning Porter was lost the moment he mentioned our *history*. He already exposed his intention to exploit my feelings for her.

Better to let him believe I only have one Achilles' heel.

He nods solemnly. "I can probably do that. Given the judge will allow a new trial, retaining another lawyer is not a problem for me. Ms. Lovell is becoming a little too difficult to work with lately, anyway."

We hit on this briefly before, but here's a reminder: Use of qualifiers—like basically, effectively, *probably*—means you're *probably* lying. See what I did there?

Shaver doesn't want to give up Porter. She's his ace up his sleeve. Not only is she a damn good defense attorney, we have history. Shaver could get quite creative using that to manipulate me.

Let's not give him that angle.

If he won't change counsel, I'll convince Porter it's in her best interest to remove herself from his case. Which, seeing as Shaver is about to go for the insanity plea, shouldn't take too much persuading. She'll want out of this circus.

Leaving Shaver all to me.

"There's one other condition to this deal," Shaver says.

"Of course. Nothing is ever simple, is it?"

His leery smile irks me. "I want you to tell me about your wife."

My hackles raise. The level of control it takes to hold an unaffected countenance strains every muscle. "I don't have a wife."

"Right. Sorry. You weren't yet married. But just the same, you lost someone, your woman, and I want to hear that story."

Yeah. Fuck this guy.

This is exactly why I can't be his doctor. I swore an oath —just as Porter swore one—to help my patients to the best of my ability. And there is nothing within me that wants to help this psycho fuck.

If that makes me unethical, so be it. That's why I'm a trial consultant and not a shrink.

"When I begin my evaluation, there won't be any mind games, Shaver. You don't get to dig around in my head to feed some twisted desire. My life—*me*—has no bearing on your diagnosis and treatment."

"So you won't tell me the story, then. Shame. Porter won't either. That just makes me all the more curious as to what the two of you are hiding."

"Do we have a deal?" I force the subject. I'm officially over this conversation, and I want Porter removed from his case today. *Now.*

Shaver holds out his hand, and the guard moves to his side. Shaver smiles. "I just want to shake on it, mate."

I stand and walk around the table. I meet his eyes, those cold orbs that have no depth, and clasp his hand. I give it a firm squeeze, eliciting another slimy smile from him, before I draw back.

To the officer, I say, "Can you please allow Ms. Lovell inside?"

"Wait."

I stare down at Shaver expectantly.

"You never asked me if I did it."

"Did you stalk, kill, and mutilate Devin Tillman?"

See? I can be blunt, too. Now who's the first to blink?

But he doesn't blink. His smile drops, and in the seconds that pass, I glimpse the truth of his intentional silence.

"Ask Ms. Lovell to come in," I say.

I keep my gaze on the man at the table as the door opens and Porter strides in.

"What did I miss?" she asks.

Finally, I look at her. And I can see what, in my miserable little cocoon I was in yesterday, I failed to acknowledge. The dark circles under her eyes that makeup can't completely conceal. The tired creases feathering her eyes.

"Do you want to tell her or should I?" Shaver says.

My mouth presses into a hard line. This isn't going to be pretty. "Mr. Shaver has fired you," I say. "Have a nice day, Ms. Lovell."

5

HARD KNOCKS

DR. IAN WEST

"God. I don't *believe* you." Porter marches ahead of me down the courthouse steps. She's fired up. No, she's pissed. I keep a good distance away from her, just in case she tries to volley her briefcase at my head.

"This is the best decision, Porter. Do you really want to tell Mathers that your client is changing his plea? To an insanity defense? That's one for the books."

She groans and whirls around as she reaches the last step. I halt before I pummel into her. "Do not patronize me," she says. "Do not *think* for me. What happened in that conference room was so far outside of right…"

"This…from the woman representing an admitted murderer?"

The seething blaze in her eyes makes me back up. Maybe that was too far. Yeah, I should leave now.

"Look," I say, chancing a step closer, because I've proven I'm not the smartest man and I don't know when to stop.

"Your *client* isn't right. Matter of fact, he's dangerous, Porter."

I have the sudden and alarming urge to sweep her hair behind her ear so I can see her eyes fully. Instead, I flex my hand by my side. Bury the urgent need to be closer to her so far down, Indiana Jones couldn't excavate it.

A group funnels down the steps. I take her arm and guide us to a more private space. A fall breeze caries her scent of lavender perfume between us, triggering memories. I inhale deeply as I look down at her, realizing we're much too close.

Porter stares up at me with a curious expression, divots line the delicate skin between her brows. What is she thinking?

That flowery, feminine scent heats my senses, a burn itching my palms. But I stand my place, baking in the fire. "I can't stand the thought of you spending one more minute with that monster," I tell her. "I need to know you're safe."

One of her rare smiles tips her mouth. "Such a hero."

"That's me. Knight in shining Armani suit."

"I don't need a knight, West. I need a friend. *My* friend. The guy who used to have my back and who trusted me to make my own choices. Whether for good or bad." She blinks up at me, the afternoon sun catching the gold currents in her eyes. "I miss that guy."

Yeah. I miss him some days, too. He was an easygoing kind of guy. He could make Porter laugh—a deep, throaty laugh that unfurled a sense of elation. I was mesmerized by her laugh.

I open my mouth to say…something, but the words are stuck in the ache clogging my throat. *What a wuss*.

It's easier being her enemy.

Her sigh wraps around me, easing some of the tension between us.

"Truthfully," she says, "it's been hard to sleep ever since this case landed on my desk." She shakes her head. "I've represented some of the worst scum of the earth, but this case...I don't know. I took an oath, and I stand by it"—she drives her point home with a severe glare—"but Quentin Shaver, he's something else. Something darker. And I know how stupid that must sound—"

"It's not stupid." I touch her now, the lightest stroke of her arm. A connection point to let her know I believe her.

"Maybe it's just stress," she amends to downplay her fear.

"I don't put a lot of stock in gut instincts. Logic is more deserving of my time." I give her a glib smile. "But the mind has a gut of its own, in a sense. I think it would be stupid to ignore its warning."

The Tarot card in my pocket feels weighty.

A faint smile graces her lips. "Fine."

I arch an eyebrow. "Fine? As in, you'll allow Shaver new representation?"

"Yup."

I cock my head, suspicious. "How painful will this be for me?"

"You owe me," she says, crossing her arms.

"Done. I owe you. Just name it, and I'll—"

"Drinks," she says, cutting me off. She circles her thin fingers around my tie, giving it a firm tug. "Tonight. You and me and a couple glasses of bourbon."

That ache lodges deeper. "Porter..."

"That's my terms. Take it or leave it."

Resigned, I nod once. "You drive a torturous bargain. You should think about trading careers altogether." I straighten my tie as she releases it. "I hear they're looking for Dominatrixes at the DA's office."

She smirks. "Funny."

As the wind picks up again, silence stretches, stacking that tension back up. Our fragile truce seems to drift away as quickly as her smile.

"I should go face the music." She checks the time on her phone. "My bosses might fire me over this."

"I doubt that."

She looks up. "How are you so sure?"

I shrug. "I know things." Like the fact that Porter was offered a partnership at her firm. She hasn't made it public yet, which makes me wonder if she's waiting until the media craze that is Shaver's case to be over.

She mouths "full of it" before she turns and heads up the courthouse steps. She pauses on the third to look back at me. "When you met with Shaver...what did you get from him?"

I sink my hands into my pockets. "Like reading him?"

She nods.

"He's guilty."

6

THE BONES

DR. IAN WEST

I met Porter first.

I was a know-it-all right out of college with my masters, and I had an interview set up with a medical research firm where I was going to show off my hotshot brain.

Porter was seated in the waiting room, her client—a disturbed young man in a bit of trouble with the law—was being evaluated. Standard court order.

"It's only my second case," she told me, when I asked about what she did.

I couldn't help myself. It was tacky to strike up a conversation in a waiting room with a sexy lawyer, but I just had this feeling... If I didn't make a move, I'd never see her again.

And I had to see her again.

When her name was called, I fought my professional nature (or lack thereof) and chased her to the glass doors, demanding that she have drinks with me that night.

I remember the pink hue that flushed her cheeks, that cute dimple, as she glanced between the receptionist and me. I wasn't leaving her alone until she agreed.

"Fine," she said. "I concede, Dr. West. Or should I just call you West?"

"You can just call me." I handed her a slip of paper with my number.

Smooth.

Needless to say, I didn't take the job. Oh, I got the offer, but the pay wasn't to my standards and I was going to have to start at the bottom in the research field. I was a snob back in the day. Still am, I guess. That's what comes with being the smartest person in the room. I was definitely smarter than my potential boss, with his crooked toupee and limp handshake.

But that's not what I remember about that day.

I remember the way Porter's dark hair caught the light with amber highlights, and bounced as she walked her little, hurried walk, her slender hips swaying hypnotically. I remember the way her nose crinkled and her golden eyes creased at the corners when she smiled.

She was…enchanting. Lame to say in this day in age maybe, but I was enchanted by her.

Later, at the bar that would become "our bar", Porter actually showed up for drinks. She had texted me that she would, but I kept watch from the bar top, staring at the door every time it opened, until the moment she walked in.

We bantered and flirted and drank two bourbons each… and had one near kiss…before she announced that she had actually made plans to meet a colleague there first, and that she hoped I didn't mind.

It was a fix up.

I'd been duped. Porter brought me there to pass me off on a friend—who was probably a real barker—and I was already scoping out my exit…until she introduced me to Melanie.

"This is my colleague, Melanie Harper."

Melanie laughed, the sound of her lilting voice encasing me in warmth that rivaled the bourbon. "You mean, partner in crime," Mel said.

And that's all it took.

I was in love.

I knew it immediately.

I'm not normally a manwhore who flits from one woman to the next (well, not now anyway), but Porter saw it, too. The way Mel and I looked at each other. She was a matchmaking goddess. Porter and I became friends, as much as any man and woman can, and Mel and I became… everything to each other.

There are many varying degrees of love. So many, in fact, that no one can experience them all in a lifetime.

I loved Melanie with my entire being. What some may refer to as a soul mate. But I also loved Porter. She was my friend, my trusted confidant.

That's what made her betrayal all the more painful.

After Mel died, I took time off. When I returned to the courtroom fold, and I saw Porter seated opposite me at the defense table, it's like another part of me withered away.

I tip my tumbler back now as I swivel on the barstool, getting sloshy drunk. The atmosphere in the industrial, downtown bar feels dry, a sort of bland nostalgia that can't quite evoke the right sentiment. Every table is taken in the quaint but hip establishment, clips of laughter adding to the rock soundtrack. The exposed ducting and beams set the urban mood, but the warm lighting and down-to-earth working class is what gives it that comfortable vibe despite all the brick, glass, and steel.

I'm seated in the same seat I was all those years ago as Porter makes her entrance.

There's a part of me still waiting for Mel to follow behind her. It's a bitter part, shriveled and hard. A little spiteful, festering nugget that despises all the couples occupying the bar.

"Just had to pick this place," I say without looking her way.

She orders a bourbon for herself, then nudges her barstool closer to mine. "I'm sentimental that way."

I bark out a laugh. This woman—who eats prosecutors for breakfast—is not sentimental. She's come a long way from the newbie attorney I met in that waiting room.

"How did Mathers take it?" I push my tumbler toward the bar edge and point at the glass. "Hit me again, my man."

The bartender has a big, bushy beard and a man bun, which makes me confident in his ability to get me nice and drunk. He serves Porter her drink and tops mine up.

"He took it," she says. "Not gracefully, of course. But I had a favor coming."

"Said like a true defense attorney." I take down a long swallow.

She impressively matches me, swallowing the amber liquid in one chug. Porter has never been one to sip when it comes to the hard stuff. "I don't know why you're so bitter," she says. "Shouldn't you be gloating? Dr. Ian West has gotten his way again. You're about to dissect one of the most confounding psychopathic minds." She smirks. "You might even get to write a paper on this. Return to your ego-inflated roots."

Touché. I set my glass down and look at her, noticing for the first time the black, low-cut dress and loose waves tumbling around her shoulders. "Got a hot date?"

"Actually, I do." She eyes me seriously. "He's a real asshole, and his ego…" She whistles.

I blow out a long breath. "What game is this, Porter? I didn't mentally prep tonight to keep up with your head games."

"No games, West." She swivels around to face me, crossing her legs in the process. My gaze lingers a little too long on the slit exposing her thigh, and she notices. "Something pique your interest?"

My gaze snaps to hers. "Did Shaver give you a card?"

Her cheery expression darkens. I hate that I just killed the smile I so rarely see on her face. But I have to know, and there's no sense in pretending this *date* is anything other than a way to work information from each other.

"What are you talking about?"

"A Tarot card," I clarify. "Did Shaver give you one?"

She tips back the rest of her bourbon, sets the glass down with finality. "No. But since you're asking, I'm assuming my client—my *former* client—" she amends "—somehow managed to give you one…for whatever reason."

"You know the reason."

She holds up a finger. "Ah. I know the *speculated* reason. And we're not going there, West. We're not drudging up every interview and witness…" She trails off, the fire in her tone draining. "I don't want to argue with you."

"Then don't."

She tilts her head. "What was the card? How do you know it was from Shaver?"

There's a whole arsenal of questions loaded in her queue just waiting to be unleashed. I take another sip and then put my glass down for good. If I'm going to do this, I need to get my head clear. And Porter's sexy dress isn't helping in that department, either.

Just acknowledging her beauty feels like a betrayal to Mel.

"Are you done with your drink?"

She downs the last dreg and plops the glass on the bar. "I am now."

"Let's go for a walk."

I hand Porter my silver flask.

"That's what I like about you," she says, as she accepts the bourbon I keep at the ready. "Always prepared. Nothing takes you by surprise. You always see them coming, and every other cliché in the book."

"I'm a cliché. Noted." I steal a peek and notice her fighting a smile.

We round the bend in the courtyard through The Yards. The waterfront park is an architect haven, with spongy green grass and a waterfall fountain that cascades into a pool where, in the summer, kids wade and splash while adults soak up the sun.

I hate being here, to be honest.

The park used to be one of our favorite places. Mel and me. We'd get a few drinks in us to warm up, walk the bricked waterfront along the railing, stare at the lights reflecting over the river. Then we'd cross the pedestrian bridge, pausing in the middle to make out like a couple of horny teens.

I don't know why I brought Porter here.

With the anniversary of Mel's death, maybe I'm just a glutton for punishment. Pile another layer of resentment on that grief ball.

Or maybe it's something deeper, darker. Uglier.

A blatant reminder of Mel, so that I get a punch to the groin every time my subconscious rears with my attraction to Porter.

If I was a mentally healthy person, I might confess that—over the past couple of years—my evolving feelings for Porter is why I've continued to keep her at arm's length. But I'm an unstable bastard, and Porter switched sides…right when I needed her the most.

"She loved it here."

Porter's words feel like a knife chiseling at my chest cavity.

I suck in a sharp breath of frigid fall air. It's all I can do. We walk along the railing, our hands tucked into our jacket pockets (thank God that sinful dress is now hidden), until we reach the grassy mound where cement benches are carved into the earth.

Porter takes a seat on the first bench and rubs her arms. "What's going on, West?"

I stare at the river, making a decision, steeling my resolve —yada yada—before I face her. "Shaver wants me to diagnose him as insane. Temporarily, that is."

She blinks up at me. "He told you this?"

"Yes." I sit down next to her. "Today in the conference room. He might be able to fool another psychologist, convince them of this. He believes he's smart enough to manipulate just about anyone, but he's also intelligent enough to know a sure thing beats a gamble. And I can tell you all this now because you're no longer his lawyer, but Porter…"

She nods. "I know. The pact."

Back in the day, when I first started my trial consulting agency, Mel, Porter, and I made a pact that what we discussed would stay among us. We were ethical, of course, but it was an impossible situation to think we'd never converse about our cases to some extent. It's what lovers and friends do, talk about their day.

"It's more than that." I groan as I shrug deeper into my jacket and pull out the Tarot card. It's still encased in the baggie, never processed. I doubt Shaver would leave fingerprints behind, but he did so once in the motel room, and there might be some other evidence planted there.

I hand it to Porter, and she studies the design on the back, then the front. "Five of Cups."

"The card depicts loss, grief." I let this sink in; she doesn't need me to spell it out. "I found it on Melanie's grave yesterday."

Porter's gaze is hard on the card. "That bastard."

I chuckle, I can't help it. "Not very ethical of you." But absolutely adorable.

She hands me the card, getting rid of it as if just holding it will contaminate her. "I know who my client is, West. There's always a well within me I reserve for hope…but someone has to do my job. Someone has to defend him."

"But not you. Not anymore."

Her nod is solemn, then she looks at me. "How did you know he was guilty?"

"His earlobes are attached."

She snorts. "Oh, come on."

"I'm serious. It's a recessive trait that is found most commonly in criminals with antisocial and psychopathic pathologies." I shrug. "Don't hate on a guy for calling it like it is."

A beat of silence fills the air where her laughter drifts off. Then she sighs. "You know, before I changed sides, after Mel died, I asked myself: Was it better to convict an innocent person or free a guilty one?"

I stare at her, watching the way the night breeze sends strands of hair across her face, the way her thick lashes fan her cheeks every time she blinks. She focuses intently on the water, as if it holds the answer.

"Well, you obviously made your choice." *No bitterness there.*

She bites her lip, then: "I never did. I don't know the answer. I started with the firm because I couldn't work at the DA's office anymore. Not without Mel."

God, I'm a dick. "Porter..." What can I say? Sorry I was so wrapped up in my own pain that I overlooked yours? I'm the guy who's supposed to know what everyone is thinking, and yet I couldn't read her.

Denial.

I didn't want to.

I was consumed with grief. I couldn't handle hers, too.

I open my mouth to say...something, but she shakes her head. "Look, I believe it's right on both sides. Someone has to prosecute, and someone has to defend. I sleep just fine at night doing what I do now. So you can put your hero cape back in the drawer."

"Again, noted. Should I bench the Superman tighty-whities, too?"

Her laugh trickles through me like a rolling clap of thunder. Surprising.

Man, I hate even more that I'm about to make it stop. "I need to know what the defense might have for exculpatory evidence in the new case. I need to know if there's proof of Shaver stalking Tillman before her murder."

Both her laugh and smile are gone. "Are you...what? Accusing me of a Brady violation?"

"No... I'd never think that about you—"

"Then you're pushing the pact too far by even asking. Your team is still helping the prosecution."

"I can read this card as a threat, Porter." I fan it between us. "Hero or not, I won't be threatened into giving Shaver an insanity defense. He's not insane."

She frowns. "You only talked to him once. For like, ten minutes. You're good, West. But even you can admit that's pushing the bounds of ethical on your part." She raises an accusatory eyebrow.

"Okay." I bring my hands out and situate myself on the bench so that I'm facing her. "How long have we been sitting here?"

"Oh no..." She goes to stand, and I seize her wrist. She glances between my hand and the river, then concedes with a sigh. "I don't want you to read me."

"I've been doing that the whole time."

A startled look flashes in her eyes.

"That look right there"—I slip my fingers to the pulse at her wrist—"the slight widening of your eyes... You're worried about what I may've uncovered during our conversation."

Her mouth twists. "You got to do better than that to impress me."

I smile. "Earlier, when I mentioned my tighty-whities, you flushed just the slightest. You had a brief image of what I might look like in those sexy briefs." I cock an eyebrow.

She laughs. "That's evil! You said that on purpose just so you could prove your point now. Humans are visual creatures. That's a given."

Her heart rate spikes. "You're lying. Which means..." I look deeper into her eyes. Her pupils dilate. "You've pictured me like that before. Maybe even naked."

Her smile falters, and she tries to remove her hand, but I keep hold. "Stop it, West. I'm not doing this."

I'm not done uncovering her secrets yet. "When you talked about your choice, whether it was better to convict or defend, you bit your lip. A telling signal that the person feels shame. You admitted you didn't know the answer to that question, which I believe. But it wasn't the question that made you feel an instance of shame, it was something else." I duck my head to find her eyes. "What's the truth, Porter?"

She sucks in a breath, then finally finds my gaze. "When I said I left because of Mel. I lied."

Dread bottoms out my stomach. "What do you mean?"

"I left because of you," she says.

Every atom in my body buzzes. A warning. *Leave.* But I can't abandon her again.

"Why?" My grip on her wrist tightens, desperate for the answer.

"West..." She bites her lip and immediately releases it. "Well for one thing, this right here. Having you always in my head...knowing what I'm thinking, feeling. It's infuriating."

Her attempt to diffuse the tension doesn't work. I hang on to her, imploring the truth. "Was it working with me? Did my sullen phase last too long?" I was a lethargic, angry man for a good while after Mel's death. No one—especially me—knew when the grieving period would end.

It never ends, by the way. It just changes. Different stages. Five stages, to be exact. Denial. Anger. Bargaining. Depression. And acceptance.

I skipped through denial, and got stuck on anger.

Every time I try to picture what the asshole who killed Mel looks like… I'm right back there.

She shakes her head. Looks away, back out to the glimmering river.

"The catch of your breath…that little intake." I draw closer to her. "Your heart is hammering. That means you're scared, Porter. And the tremble of your lips tells me that you're preparing to tell the truth, that you don't want to lie, despite the fear." I clasp her chin and pull her face toward me, so I can see her eyes. "You can tell me the truth."

"Can I? What kind of person would that make me if I say it aloud?"

The suspense is doing a number on my head.

"I was scared," she admits.

"Of what?"

"That I wouldn't be able to hide my feelings for you without Mel there. And God, I loathed myself for that, West. Trust me, I still do. But I never, not once, harbored any jealousy. You two were my ideal—I envied what you had, and I loved you and her for having it. But without Mel as a buffer to keep my feelings suppressed…" She trails off, leaving the rest unsaid. But I know what belongs in that blank.

She stares down at my hand that's still wrapping her wrist. Her pulse speeds, thumping against the pads of my fingers, triggering my own heart rate to jack. I push the words past the ache in my throat. "When?"

Just one word, and maybe not the best follow-up to her confession, but she latches on to the meaning.

"You know, for all your abilities, you're pretty unobservant when it comes to women." She finally pulls free of my hand, and I let her. "The waiting room, West. That's when."

All this time, and I'm an idiot.

I was convinced that Porter invited Mel that night because she wasn't interested in me—that I wouldn't take a hint. And it worked out spectacularly.

But that's more convenient for me, isn't it?

Then I went MIA when Melanie died. I couldn't look at Porter without seeing Mel's face; the memories too painful. My grief is an asshole.

"You don't have to say anything," she says. "It is what it is. But I can't let my feelings cloud my judgment. I can't give you inside information on the case."

Yeah. Because that would make me king of the assholes.

"But I can tell you that, if Shaver really did give you a Tarot card, you should withdraw as an expert witness." She looks at me then, her golden eyes shimmering with the lights of downtown. "Get Eddie off the case, too. Let another ADA prosecute."

"I'm not giving Shaver a get-out-of-jail-free card." My mouth flattens. "Sorry for the pun. I'm not letting another doctor get on that stand and declare him insane, Porter. When he pleads innocent, I want to look into his eyes as I testify to his premeditation. I know how his mind works, and I want the whole world to know it, too."

She frowns. "Your vanity always did get the better of you."

"This isn't vanity." I tilt my head, shrug. "Okay. Not entirely. I do like to be right—but Shaver is a sadistic predator who stalks and mutilates his victims and evades authority over and over." I take her hand. "Be on my side on this one."

"West…"

"No. For three years I've watched you defend the dregs of society, and for what? Because 'someone has to do it'? Bullshit. You just admitted it was more personal than that. So…" I lace our fingers together. "Come back."

Her hand trembles in mine. Her gaze seeks to latch on to something other than me, avoiding. I keep pushing.

"Come back to us, Porter. You don't belong there." I palm her cheek, my skin aflame at touching her, feeling her. How have I been so fucking clueless? "I can't do this without you."

A tear slips down her cheek, and I swipe it away with my thumb. "I can't… I have to think about it." Her hand covers mine against her face before she pulls away. "It's late. I need sleep. I need a clear head."

"Right." I clear my throat. As she stands, I say, "I'm interviewing Shaver to give a preliminary diagnosis. But I'm firm on this. When I take the stand, Shaver is going to be put away."

She nods, solemn. "I'm not asking for anything," she says, wrapping her jacket tighter against the wind as she stares at the river. "I know right from wrong. I know there are lines we don't cross. But if I don't do this at least once…"

She looks back at me, and—before I can take my next breath—she moves in. Her soft lips capture mine, taking me by surprise, and all I can do is taste her, inhale the sweetness of the kiss, before she pulls away.

That near kiss in the bar…

Would things have been different if I'd known how Porter felt?

I can't think that way.

"Another thing I like about you," she whispers against my mouth, "your convictions. See you tomorrow."

Dumbfounded, I watch her walk off. There's an overwhelming ache in my chest, but it's not painful. It feels too full, overpowering. Then I glance at the bridge, and the damn niggling of shame sets in. A guilty pang when I remember Melanie.

For just a brief moment, she was gone. Out of mind. I forgot her.

"Dammit."

I pull my jacket closed and make the trek to my apartment building, self-loathing in full swing. I just asked Porter to join our team. Where I'll have to see her every day.

Where I can't escape her.

And I don't even know what I feel.

Or what I've done.

When I get inside my apartment, I crank the heat and bury myself in a healthy dose of bourbon to bring on a blackout.

7

SHUFFLE THE DECK

DR. IAN WEST

Know what's worse than evaluating a psychopathic serial killer? Evaluating a psychopathic serial killer while nursing a hangover.

Or maybe that's a trick question. There's nothing worse, either way, and that's precisely why I didn't make it a full year at my starter career as a forensic psychologist before Melanie suggested I come at it from a different angle.

"This is a little outside your qualifications, isn't it, Dr. West?"

I smile—nice and big—at Shaver's new defense attorney. He went with a real douchebag this time in Steve Smigel. I mean, really. Smigel? That's a few letters removed from The Lord of the Rings troll. Might as well call him Gollum. And I do, in my head.

"It was at your client's request, Smigel." *Gollum.* "Take it up with him." Because there are many other places I'd rather be right now. Like in bed, covers piled over my head, avoiding Porter.

Or in bed with Porter.

I shake the thought away. *Down boy.*

Alcohol and nostalgia never mix well.

"I'm just saying," the troll continues, "there's no jury here. How long has it been since you actually did real psychology work instead of just jury consulting?"

Just jury consulting. As if what I do isn't real. *Amateur.* "Trial science," I correct him, and he raises a wiry eyebrow. "That's the proper terminology. You know, just so you don't sound uneducated, being that you've worked in the field of law for all of—?" I pretend to think.

"A year," he provides.

"Ah, right. Do they still hand out lollipops to first years over at Marks and Vasier?"

His scowl gives me great satisfaction.

I crack open my briefcase on the table, fastening one eye closed as the resounding *clack* ricochets around my pounding head. Forty-five minutes of looking professional and then I can get out of here.

Smigel steps aside as a guard enters the room, and I hear the scraping clang of chains as another officer escorts Shaver inside. The second officer seats Shaver at the table across from me and fastens the handcuff chain to the manacle in the center of the table.

This is not the original table in the conference room. This table was transported from the nearby correctional facility just for Shaver. Rather than taking any risk transporting Shaver back and forth before his new trial date, the judge ordered to keep him here under heavy guard.

Shaver's gaze doesn't stray from me as the guard checks

and rechecks his restraints. Then he moves to stand at the door. A motionless, fixed sentinel keeping watch.

I wait for the first guard to take Smigel out of the room before I relax into the chair. Since Shaver got special privileges, it was only fair that I get some of my own. I had Charlie drop off my office chair, and then it was this whole ordeal to get approval…but it was worth it. The superior cloud that always hovers around Shaver has been doused a fraction.

"Like my chair?" I give it a spin, planting my feet to stop when facing him again.

"It's lovely, Dr. West," he says, his irritating accent clipped in that haughty way of his.

"Sure beats your table," I say. "Maybe next time they can bring you a leather reclining restraint bench, too. Then we'll be equals. Do they make those?" I smile smugly.

He sits forward and clasps his hands together, as much as the handcuffs will allow. "That's an interesting musing. Us as equals."

I stop swiveling my chair. "You don't think we are?"

"Is this question part of your evaluation?"

I smile. "Shaver, I started evaluating you the first day of the trial. Force of habit, being a psychologist and all. Hard to flip the switch."

His eyes narrow, lips parted in a peculiar half-smile. "Flip the switch. I like that. Something that is so inherently ingrained in us is difficult to turn off."

"That would be my meaning."

"I wonder how difficult it is, then, to be around Ms. Lovell. All her little idiosyncrasies to dissect."

I do not like his use of her name and "dissect" in the same sentence. To which he knows, as his smile widens.

Time to cook this bastard.

I flip a manila file open on the table and pick up a pen. I recite the date out loud, followed by my name and credentials. Then I look at Shaver. "This commences the start of your official evaluation, Quentin Shaver, as so ordered by The Superior Court of the District of Columbia." I reach over and push Pause on the video recorder. "I'm here as agreed, but our deal is null and void should you mention Ms. Lovell again. Understood?"

"Understood, Dr. West." He gives me his most intimidating, penetrating stare. "A man is only as good as his word. A broken agreement… Well, that's inexcusable."

Smug bastard. I get the message. Don't cross him. "While we're still in a time out, I have a question."

"Go ahead."

"Why change your plea mid trial? As far as I could tell, the trial was going your way."

His expression—that is usually so calm—falters. A twitch of insecurity, then a flash of anger. A little snarl of the top lip. But we have to be careful not to read too much into these microexpressions with Shaver. He's practiced in controlling his features. If I'm seeing his conveyed emotions, I have to wonder if it's because he wants me to.

How's that for a mind fuck?

God, I hate evaluating psychopaths.

"To date, how many cases have you lost for your clients?" he asks.

My turn to be smug. "None."

Which is the truth. But to be fair, and to add a slice of humble pie to my ego, I don't accept losing cases. I and my team evaluate every aspect before we agree to take on a client. Even Eddie has had cases rejected when I knew there was a chance for a loss.

It's not that I fear a challenge. Every case presents its own challenges.

It's the sage choice career wise. In DC, the heart of government, who wants to hire a trial consulting agency that loses? *Never lost* makes for damn good marketing.

Then to a lesser extent, there is that slight thing of believing in your clients. A piece of Mel I keep alive in the company.

"I want to be on the winning side," Shaver says. "And that's any side you're on, Dr. West."

Stroke my ego a bit more there, buddy. "You didn't know about Rendell's phone," I surmise the truth.

He releases a lengthy sigh. I take it as a form of admission. "The weak are so easy to crack. I'd rather put my fate in your hands than hers."

Duly noted. I hit Record and start the interview.

I get through the routine questions—home life, parents, family, upbringing—to which Shaver answers predictably. He must have studied the cliff notes to the insane serial killer's handbook.

He denies any abuse. He refutes having harmed animals as a child. He projects empathy, displaying no psychopathic traits. I truly believe he can fool the system.

One last question: "Why did you kill and mutilate Devin Tillman?"

Now, the typical reply to a question like this by your average deranged murderer would be to supply one of the following: Denial, or brag.

Since Shaver has already arranged a new plea of innocent by way of insanity, he can't very well deny the murder. So it stands to reason that he'd go into detail at this point, laminating on the particulars to relive the kill. Even admit to other murders, if he's so bold.

Many killers have inflated the number of their victims. Once caught and incarcerated, number of kills gives them clout in prison. Also media attention. If you're going to go down as a sadistic killer, might as well go down in history.

But here's where it gets interesting.

Shaver's response: "I don't know."

I look up from my notes. "What happened the evening leading up to the murder?" I will not downplay it by referring to it as *the event*. More so for the benefit of those who will evaluate the interview later rather than for Shaver.

"You won't believe me," he says.

"Try me."

Eyes unblinking, stare intent, he says, "I was trying to save her."

Ah. Now I get it. I've been waiting for the tee up, where Shaver would reveal what particular psychopathy he's trying to adapt for his defense. You know I'm bored when I use a *golf* reference. "Please, continue."

"The demons were eating her alive from the inside out," he says. He's so calm, so deliberate. I'm convinced that, while delivering this speech, he believes his own lies. He has to in order to convey this level of sincerity with a straight face. "The only way to save her was to set them free, to cut them out."

For the laymen, just a bit of clarity: There's a difference between psychopathy and psychosis. While psychopathy is any personality disorder of the antisocial variety, psychosis exhibits a loss of reality, either long or short term, such as with brief psychotic disorder. And usually has a major stressor to induce a sudden onset. Hallucinations, delusions, erratic behavior—all symptoms. Conveniently for Shaver.

See, psychopathy is incurable. But a state of psychosis—one not linked to a mental illness such as schizophrenia (though my money was on that)—can be treated, corrected. There's a chance for rehabilitation with medication and therapy and…here's the kicker… eventual release. Set back into the wild.

And how might one pull this off?

Trauma. Brain damage.

All I have to do is go along with it and not look for the source, and Shaver gets a reduced sentence and a nice stay in a mental ward, a couple of scripts, and early release when he's declared sane.

But why would I do this? That's the question, isn't it? Porter has been removed from the case, and the only threat made to my person was a Tarot card on my dead fiancé's grave. Sent by a psychopath behind bars who targets innocent women.

I'm not seeing it, asshole.

I reach into my inseam pocket, and the guard—who I honestly forgot was still in the room—makes a move forward. "Just a card," I tell him, and hold it up so he can examine it. Then I lay it on the table. "Can you explain this to me, Shaver?"

Vague. Putting the ball in his court. How far does he want to take this?

I watch his face, looking for the flare of nostrils, widening of eyes in acknowledgement, the twitch of his lips as he tries to hide his pleasure in getting a response from me. Although having Melanie's gravesite invaded did anger me, I'm playing up that anger for Shaver's benefit. I want to crack him, discover his tell.

"It's a Tarot card, Dr. West," he answers simply.

"I see that." I tap the card with two fingers. "What I want to know is what it means to you."

He sits forward and reaches toward the card, chain scraping the table. His fingers skim the plastic covering reverently. "When I was a boy, there was this old gypsy lady who lived down the road. The kids made fun of her. Egged her house. Played doorbell ditch, I think is the American term? Anyway, the parents told us to stay away, to leave the poor lady alone."

He turns the card so that it's right-side up, the cloaked man facing me. "Even then," he continues, "before I understood the world, I felt this presence about her. This old-world knowledge. She approached me one day and the kids ran away, but I stood my ground. She drew a card from her pocket and rested it against my forehead and said: 'The man in the cloak will be your salvation.'"

I can feel my features crease as I just stare at him. I'm sure I'm giving my speculation away, as he's studying me just as intently, yet I don't care. I'm thoroughly confused as to whether this is an embellishment to further his claim of a delusional state, or if it's the truth. Either way, I jot a quick note to check if this woman is still alive—and if not, when and *how* she died.

"How old were you?" I ask.

"Thirteen. The age of enlightenment." His smile doesn't reach his eyes.

"What did you think she meant by this?"

He shrugs. "Then, I couldn't tell you. Just that I was special, and possibly that some dark figure in a cloak, though my young mind saw him as a super hero with a cape—" he chuckles "—was coming for me." He sniffs hard and sits straighter. "Or maybe the Grim Reaper."

And there's your inflated sense of self, folks. His true psychopathy is finally slipping through.

"But he couldn't be the Grim Reaper if he was meant to save me," Shaver says. "I thought about it over the years, deciding it was metaphorical. You know how you have that one defining moment when you're young? Something profound that always resurfaces?" I nod so he'll move the fuck on. "The gypsy and her prophecy was it for me."

"This is why you became invested in the Arcana," I say, the question implied.

He shows his teeth—not quite a smile or sneer. "Yes. This moment in my life had a major impact. I learned to read the cards, to trust their insight."

"And use the Tarot as your selection process."

I'm skirting the safety line here, inferring a *victim* selection process. But Shaver is smart enough to run with it. He can give me a truthful answer while not incriminating himself simultaneously.

His gaze narrows. "I saw Devin in the cards," he says, going along with it. "I saw her pain. Her suffering. So when she came to me, I couldn't deny her. I gave her a reading, and that's when the cards revealed the demon inside her. She clawed at her skin, begging for release. And I just…"

"Snapped?" I offer.

He nods slowly. "I saw myself…" He closes his eyes. "Cutting into her flesh, carving around the bone. Cracking the breastplate to get to her heart, because the heart is what needed to be set free. I felt it pumping in my hands as I held it, but it was as if I was watching from the outside, like a dream. The blood...so much of it...painted my hands. So red, just like the figure on her card. The release of red would free her, and I couldn't stop myself. Her pain was infectious. I had to make it stop."

Weaving truth into your fiction is an excellent way to create a believable lie. Tillman probably was clawing at her skin. With need for a fix. But Shaver's "snapped" explanation will never sit well with a jury. Especially a jury that I help select.

"You said she had a card. Where is that card now?"

If he answers truthfully, this could give us a starting point to uncover the Tarot link in other cases. Unlike most serial killers that have a clear MO, Shaver's is more difficult to deduce. Mutilation is a common compulsion, for varying reasons. If he removed the heart of every victim, that would be a common denominator, at least. But the search Charlie has been conducting using ViCAP and other law enforcement databases hasn't pinged that MO.

If the Tarot shows Shaver his victims, then it's a logical assumption that he has a predetermined, selective kill method for each. I make a note to have Charlie search for victims who are missing organs. Maybe cases overlooked to be serial in nature due to their black market appeal.

Shaver's mask slips for a second, and I glimpse the calculated way he's assessing me. It sends an uncomfortable chill up my spine. "The cards always return to the deck, Dr. West," he finally answers.

I glance down at the bagged card on the table. This is a card from Shaver's personal deck, and he's telling me that—after he's through with me—the card will be returned.

I pocket the card and close the folder before I turn off the camera. "I'll order the MRI and CAT scan." Then I stand.

"Are we done, Dr. West?"

"We're done," I say. "Once I get the test results, I'll have my evaluation completed and delivered to your attorney." I snap my briefcase shut. If there is trauma to the brain, I will eat my tie. How Shaver expects me to take the stand and boldface lie about a brain scan... Well, something is amiss here.

Mia's comment about proceeding cautiously tickles my thoughts.

Shaver's disappointment is evident in his wayward expression, a hint of defiance peering through. He needs to be in control of this interview and this process.

Not happening.

As I pause at the door, awaiting the guard to unlock it, Shaver gets in one last word. "Don't you want to know your reading, Dr. West? What the Five of Cups has in store for you?"

Okay, so maybe it's more than one word. But it all sounds like a string of nonsense to me. "No." I exit the room.

Before the door closes, I hear Shaver say, "You will."

Nice bit of foreboding there, right? Creepy fucker.

Outside the courthouse, I take out my phone to call Porter, to give her an update...then think better. The less she's involved, the safer for her.

At least, this is the plausible excuse not to talk to her. The other half of me is just chicken shit after what she said the night before. Hangover curbed, I call Eddie instead. "You want the good or the bad?"

"Shit. Is there really any good?"

"No."

He calls me a crude name, and I laugh. "Shaver is lining

up a psychosis defense." This psychobabble means nothing to him, so I explain. "He'll get out in two years."

"Dammit." After a few tense seconds, he says, "What if we do what narcotics couldn't?"

"I'm intrigued. What are you thinking?"

"Manslaughter might not carry the same weight as murder in the first, but it's easier to prove. And with Shaver's profession…"

"Gives credence to his sudden psychosis." His *snapped* defense. "All you'd have to do is convince the jury a street drug could induce a state of psychosis." Which given Shaver's notorious reputation, may actually work.

It's not how I'd like to take Shaver down, but sometimes you settle. For the greater good.

"All I'd have to do?" Eddie echos, a chuckle in his voice. "Sure thing, doc."

"Come on, now. Spoiled rich kids always get their way."

"Yeah. And sometimes, they get disbarred."

8

THE LOVERS

DR. IAN WEST

There's nothing romantic about the justice system. It's a slow-moving organism with a callus shell formed by years of unwavering burden.

And it's expensive.

The process to get Shaver a new trial is a slow crawl with many lashings. Eddie takes a beating—but not as bad as the one taken by the defense. After today, I think Porter may be plotting my demise.

And even though I'm not technically on any one side as a trial consultant, I've caught Judge Mathers giving me the stink-eye during court today.

Hey, what can I say? I bring out the best in everyone.

The evidence remains the same. But everything else changes. The players switch positions like a game of musical chairs. Eddie is no longer trying to prove Shaver's guilt, rather he's now—with my team's help—building a case to convict on a state of advanced inebriation, and to disprove the defense's claim of temporary insanity.

Porter's had her wrist slapped by her firm and has been benched for two weeks. I'm not sure what this means for her promotion as a partner, or what it means for us… But I'd like to think—even if she loathes me for it—that she's being protected.

She's far enough out of harm's way that I can almost reason clearly again.

Almost.

Porter did a number on my head. But I can't think about that right now.

The pews are filled with my favorite kind of people.

Potential jurors.

I recline back and sprawl my arms along the backing of the pew. The woman next to me coughs loud enough to indicate I'm invading her precious, personal space.

"Sorry," I whisper, as I tuck my limbs back in.

It's time for *voir dire*—where I shine. For me, this is where the case is either won or lost.

Jury selection is a science. Yet it's not so much selecting jurors as it is eliminating them. Before the first trial, we made a composite of what our ideal juror would look like. Not physically, but personality wise.

This person would have no reservation in convicting Quentin Shaver.

The biggest prerequisite: They must have no bias against the death penalty.

But Shaver isn't being tried for the death penalty, you say. The concept is the same. A person who has strong convictions about theories like "an eye for an eye" are the people we want. They have zero tolerance for injustice.

And if we can find those twelve people… (oh, in a perfect trial!), then we're halfway there. Since Shaver's trial is based around his admission of guilt, these people would have a difficult time believing in his demon delusion and insanity defense.

But these same people would totally get behind a drug lord's drug-induced mania where he stalks Tillman to a motel and proceeds to torture, bind, and stab her eight times, then slice up her corpse and remove her heart.

The details are gory. But those details are significant to the trial. Our ideal jurors will revolt against a system that lets an animal like that walk around free.

I sent my updated specs on the ideal juror to Mia and Charlie this morning through secure email. Charlie is waiting in the wings for the first name to investigate.

Since we don't have access to the jury list (that would be illegal) to investigate potentials beforehand, we have just minutes to investigate a juror and make the call whether to keep or cut them.

It's exhilarating.

While Mia and Eddie and I are working the *voir dire* angle, I need someone working the narrative angle. This person needs to buddy up to the case detective…and man, that's not going to be an easy alliance. For either party.

Defense attorney and Major Crimes? Working together?

Doesn't happen. Detectives work with prosecutors.

But I have to have Porter on my side. No matter where we stand personally, she belongs on the team. And I need her.

Which is why I've sneakily sicced Mia on Porter to convince her it's time to return to the fold.

Don't judge. I already admitted what a wuss I am when it comes to Porter. And that kiss… I might as well revoke my

Man Card. It sent me right into hiding behind my work where it's safe.

The judge calls the court's attention to the first potential juror to begin *voir dire*. "Thank God," I breathe. One more minute stuck in this thought pattern and I'd ram my head against the front pew.

"You called…" Mia says in my earpiece.

"Funny." I give the woman next to me a smile, and she inches farther away.

"Clarisse is up first," I whisper, and think better about making a Hannibal joke.

"I know it's killing you not to go there," Mia remarks. "Okay, we're on it."

My foot taps anxiously as I wait.

"Clarisse Boyer." Mia's back. "Charlie didn't dig too deep into her. At thirty-three, she's an insurance broker. Single. No children. Hobbies include movies and reading. But her biggest hobby is participating in the local correctional facility's pen pal program."

I scrub a hand down my face. I know why Charlie didn't dig any further after that. "Let me guess. Obsessive savior complex."

"That. Or she's just obsessed with criminals in general. I think it's more of a danger element. Get close to the fire type deal."

When it comes to the behavioral side of things, I trust Mia's insight. A woman infatuated with criminals and danger doesn't belong on this jury. And a Clarice joke is just way too easy now. Shame.

Smigel asks the potential a few key questions, getting a beat on her, then looks at the judge. "The defense accepts this juror, Your Honor."

Yeah, of course you do. She'd serve you up a hot dish of innocent verdict soup.

Eddie glances back at me, and I rub my nose. Our code for: *cut the juror*. Eddie stands. "I move to strike this juror, Your Honor."

Now, a peremptory challenge or strike is the right for both the prosecution and defense to reject a juror without a reason. Each side gets to challenge ten jurors, as this is a first degree murder case, just FYI.

That may seem like a lot, but those strikes go quicker than you'd think.

Smigel moves to question the next potential. "Next up is Andrew Smith."

The line stays quiet for so long, I get nervous. "Mia?"

"Sorry. I'm here. Okay, Andrew Smith. Charlie says everything checks out. History teacher at the local high school. Not a lot of online activity, though. That's where we got held up. His social media accounts are dormant. He doesn't spend a lot of time online. Probably to avoid his students."

"Ten/four." I think as I study the man sitting in the gallery. *Think. Think.* With no online imprint, I'm not sure which way he's swaying. Every juror comes into court with a predisposition, an opinion. Having a background on their political views and bias helps us discover this before trial.

I motion at Eddie to ask Smith our death penalty question.

Smith's reply: "If a person is proven guilty of an atrocious crime, having taken a life…then the punishment should fit the crime. I'm for it."

Damn. So perfect. Still, I hesitate. Eddie glances at me, eyebrows raised in question. A teacher would make an ideal foreman, and with an opinion like that…

I nod once.

"This juror is acceptable to the prosecution, Your Honor."

Off to a good start. I get comfortable. We still have a ways to go, and the next potential proves that with her disdain for everything on this planet.

"Tell me the rest of the pool doesn't look this bleak," I whisper.

By the recess, I'm camped out on the courthouse steps. Shoulders slouched, head hung in defeat. At least it feels like a minor defeat at the midway stage. Four jurors. That's how many we have so far that I can reasonably say won't let Shaver off on an insanity defense.

With five potentials to question, one strike left, and two seats to fill, our odds are dwindling.

I feel her presence before she says anything. Porter takes up the seat beside me, her lavender scent invading my senses and making my heart beat faster.

"It would've been easier to take him down with a guilty verdict during the first trial," I admit out loud.

"Wow. Thanks," she says. "Why don't you tell me how you really feel about my skills."

"That's not what I meant." I release a sigh. "I was worried about going up against you. Again." I peek at her. "You're tough to beat. Damn near impossible these days."

"You've done a damn good job of it."

That stings. It may be true that I've helped my clients win against Porter over the past few years, and I may have even done so a bit more personally than professionally—but I always kept the reason I'm doing this front and center.

"It's not about the win, Porter," I say, regardless of what I lead the world to believe. "It's about justice." It's about Mel, and her murderer—the scum hit-and-run driver that I will never be able to punish. When I look into the eyes of a defendant and I see their guilt..

They become that person. They're *all* that person. And I make damn sure they don't go free.

She nods solemnly. "I know, West. But there's a balance to keep. Just like Shaver. He can't be convicted on one opinion. That's why there are twelve people to debate their opinions. Not just yours."

"People are predictable. You can paint the picture in black and white, and they'll still see gray."

She shakes her head. "No one wants to think that they could wake up one day and just suddenly mutilate a person. They believe they would have to be crazy, temporary or otherwise, in order to do something so heinous."

She's a smart cookie. "Even with Shaver's not so innocuous media presence, he's built a reputation around drugs, not murder. Which is quite brilliant, to be honest. A jury would be ready to convict on a drug charge."

Which is why we have the backup drug angle.

"I have faith in you." Porter nudges my arm. "I wasn't looking forward to battling you in court either, by the way."

More bold than I feel at the moment, I look into her eyes. "You don't have to." The meaning of my statement lingers in the crisp fall air between us.

"Mia called me." She straightens her back, angling her knees toward me. I have the urge to reach over and lay my hand on her thigh. It's such a natural reaction, it scares me.

"She misses you," I say.

"If I consider this…" Braver than me, she does reach

over. She takes my hand and places it right on her knee, lacing her fingers over mine. "I need to know where we stand, West. Not now. Not even this week. But soon. I'm not giving my notice at the firm and walking into a virtual emotional landmine that's going to explode in both our faces." She tilts her head, gaze intent. "Can you handle that?"

Damn. One kiss and I'm a dead man.

"Three years," I hear myself say. "That's a long time, Porter."

She shrugs. "Don't get your super ego going. It's not like I waited around, staring out my window all forlorn and shit." I laugh, and she graces me with one of her rare smiles. "I dated. I moved on. But it just so happens that I'm sick of trying to get over the one that got away."

I open my mouth to say something, but she holds up a finger.

"Wait. Let me get this out." Deep breath. "If we don't talk about it, we'll always have the elephant in the room. We both love Mel. And we both want to honor her memory, and that means this—" she motions between us "—has to be said out loud."

A sick pang fires through my stomach. But I know the truth. I know what Mel would say; I know that she would give her blessing to the two people she loved, but that doesn't mean it makes me feel any less guilty.

"She would want you to be happy, West." She sneaks a glance at me. "I can feel guilty, you can feel guilty…we can both feel like guilty assholes, but that would be us and our issues. Not her. Never from her."

I nod, even though I can't look at her. Admitting something out loud is different than facing it.

Porter squeezes my hand. "I'm ready, West. I'm ready to

try, no matter what we risk if we fail. It has to be better than being your enemy."

I could make a case that we'd risk our friendship, but the pathetic truth is we haven't been friends since Mel died. I let the pain set the course for us, and I did make her the enemy.

"I kind of like getting you fired up in court, though," I say. "I think it helps you win cases."

Shock crosses her face. "Unbelievable. You take credit for everything."

"Only the good stuff."

Her gaze lingers on our hands. "Then I'll try not to hold the past three years against you."

Right in the gut. She knows where to hit. I not only kept her at arm's length, I pushed her off the side of my planet. I let her decision to go to the dark side (the defense's side – ha!) become an excuse to stay angry with her. It's so much easier to feel that anger than it is to feel that hurt.

Hey, I am a psychologist. I can be self-aware when I need to.

"I don't want to break your heart." It just comes out. I hate myself for voicing it, but she has to know the truth. That I'm still a bitter, resentful asshole, and chances are, I'd fuck this up.

"Let me worry about my heart. You worry about the case. Now, I can't technically work with you on anything that was in discovery in the previous case, but I can look for new evidence. Do I have an assignment yet?"

"Whiplash?" I try to laugh it off, but I'm caught. She won't let me wriggle out of this. "I need someone to work with Major Crimes."

She nods knowingly. "Detective Renner is the case

detective." She gives a light whistle. "I can't say that she likes me much."

"But you'd be gathering facts for the prosecution. She might dislike Shaver even more, don't you think?"

"Good point." She checks her phone, then stands. "I'll work on Renner during my probation period at the firm. Two weeks. That should give you time to think it through."

Watching her walk away is the highlight of my day. That damn pencil skirt does a number on my arteries. I palm my chest, feeling the *thump* speed. Porter commands respect with an equal measure of feminine sensuality.

And she drives me crazy.

God, Mel—please don't let me fuck this up.

9

OF HEART AND MIND

DR. IAN WEST

Let's talk about change for a moment. More specifically, the ability to change.

I see you checking the time…looking for an escape route. Any time the topic of change is brought up (and it is quite often in therapy; hence why people dislike therapy), our immediate reaction is to throw up defenses.

I can't change. I am who I am.

This is one of the most painful subjects to tackle. Because it usually revolves around pain itself.

As a species, we are defined by our pain. It's not the good and fun and easy moments that form our personality. If that was the case, we'd all be a bunch of lazy slugs lounging on the beach, drinking Mai Tais and toasting the good life. Blissfully unaware of tragedy and hardship.

We'd also be boring as fuck.

Every adversity we conquer teaches us more about ourselves. Our strength, preservation, our intelligence and capacity to learn and grow, so that we can face the next challenge. So forth and so forth.

Along the way, stumbling down life's road of razor and fire, we're sharpened, we're forged. We're given depth, and compassion. We recognize this intrinsic pain in others and we commiserate. We bond together in order to *not do it alone*.

Life is pain.

Probably one of the oldest sayings. Does anyone even know who first stated this? I think it needs an update: Life is shared pain.

No one—no one is an island. But if you're unable to connect through your pain, you can become a conditioned island of bitter misery.

I'm getting off topic. The point is, whether pain is mental or physical, we are molded by our experiences. Most profound moments happen during our most trying experiences. And pain teaches us to adapt.

Change is not only possible, it is inevitable.

And, of course! There's a term for this: Neuroplasticity. Or brain plasticity, is our brain's ability to change throughout our life.

It's sort of an umbrella term, as there are many stages and definitions depending on your specialty. But to make it easier for this lesson, I'm only going to focus on me. I'm a bit egotistical that way—but it is my story.

I'm seated at a table in a restaurant. Surrounded by friends and colleagues.

We're celebrating the end of *voir dire*, and the fact that we managed to gain six jurors in our favor. No small feat, considering the pool. The truth is, people are becoming more sensitive, understanding, forgiving (thanks, millennials).

Cultural Neuroplasticity at work—if there was such a thing—would be a perfect example. Not so good for our case.

Mia and Charlie came through to deliver two more jurors with their epic teamwork dynamic. A fusion of behavioral science and investigative skills that make the top dogs in law enforcement green with envy. I pride myself that I hired them both first. Yes, I'll take the credit.

M and C are already hard at work building a mock jury. Twelve people that have similar values and beliefs, where we can simulate the trial and discover what will sway the remaining six jurors. It's not as unethical as it sounds. People want to have their beliefs challenged. They want to be shocked and awed amid a trial. Reality TV at its finest minus the TV. And what's more, they ultimately want to do the right thing.

Shocking, I know. But people, for the most part, are inherently good. It takes a lot of vileness to want to inflict pain and unnecessary punishment on another human being. Shared pain, remember? To commiserate is in our nature.

Our part is to help the jury do what they are already designed to do: have mercy.

But not for the defendant.

For the victim.

Mercy and justice for Devin Tillman, the woman who was stalked, abducted, and tortured in a motel room for hours, while friends and family assumed she was just off on another drug binge.

Eddie, having already taken a crack at trying Shaver during the first (partial) trial, knows what he's up against. Shaver is a master manipulator. Everyone thinks they're unswayable. That they're smarter than average, and incorruptible. That if they were in the jury hot seat, they would punish the bastard.

It's the same logic that comes into play when you're at a grocery store and witness an exhausted mother trying to console a whiny, intolerant child.

I would punish my child. I would never allow my child to behave like that in public, so you say.

Everything is always so easy and clear from the grass on the other side of the fence. Why, yes, I do like mixing (butchering) metaphors. Stop judging. You're only proving my point.

Back on topic: When it's you in the hot seat, and a person's freedom or even their very life is in your hands… The clarity of the situation becomes muddled. We are innately wired to commiserate with other human beings (that shared pain thing again), and therefore, when placed on a jury to judge, we in turn pull inward, placing ourselves in the accused's place.

Because, hey, it could just as easily happen to us. And what about doubt? Years later DNA and yada yada proved someone served a life sentence that was really innocent. How can you be 100% sure he's guilty? How could you live with yourself if you put an innocent man away for life?

If you're human, and have a smidgen of empathy, you couldn't live with yourself.

So the easier, less distressing verdict is always *not guilty*.

It's why you're so shocked a jury let someone free who you just *knew* was guilty.

This is the psychology of the justice system.

Like Porter voiced, nearly every person serving in the field of law battles this exact conundrum—to try to figure out their place; which side of the coin they're on.

CARDS OF LOVE | 87

Long ago (maybe not that long; like back in the 1700s or something; I didn't pay attention that day in class), a guy named Blackstone touted it for the masses, to simplify the challenge of guilt verses innocence. And the masses took to it, grateful, for they didn't have to struggle any more with the moral dilemma.

The Blackstone ratio states: It is better that ten guilty persons escape than that one innocent suffer. In other words, if there's even an ounce of doubt, set the bastard free. Blackstone didn't invent the ratio, he might've borrowed it from the Bible, but the logic is clear, simple, and it's been a staple in law for centuries. Our very justice system is built around it.

Without the full vote of twelve jurors to judge Shaver as guilty of murder, he will get his reasonable doubt. He will be proven not guilty by reason of insanity.

Unless…there's a twist.

Juries love a good twist in the narrative of a trial.

"I still don't understand how the defense is calling you as an expert witness," Eddie remarks, breaking into my thoughts. To be continued.

That is the question, isn't it? The enigma. Is Shaver so certain in his ability to fool a jury that he's willing to chance putting me on the stand, or does his confidence lie somewhere else—like fate—like the Tarot card I carry in my pocket. Its meaning, and threat, still a mystery.

"Is Shaver deceptive or delusional?" I question out loud.

Eddie's strikingly blond, slicked-backed hair is extra gelled tonight, I notice. He wipes his mouth with a cloth napkin. "Are you asking me?"

I glance around the booth at the team.

Mia raises her hand. "Both," she says. "In order to make

others believe his lies, he has to believe them, which makes him delusional to an extent."

I tap my nose. "He's been trying to get inside my head. The Tarot card, talking about Melanie—" this gets a sympathetic frown from Eddie—"so next he'll target all of you. Anyone close to me, he'll allude to threats. That's why I'm being called," I explain. "Deceptively, and delusionally, he thinks I can be controlled on the stand."

"Should we be worried?" Charlie asks.

As a cop's son, his first instinct is to report a threat. But Shaver's already behind bars. The authorities can't protect any of us from this type of intimidation, which is only psychological at this point. Not to say Shaver's reach can't extend outside his bars; I believe that's the point he was trying to make by having the card placed on Mel's gravesite. Just saying that you can't work in law and buckle at every psychopath's threat.

Besides, as far as Shaver's associates will know, my team is off the ADA's case. "From here on out, you're all fired."

Shock is my colleagues. Mia's blood-red lips twist in confusion. Then Charlie reacts. "Dr. West, this is highly unfair."

I hold up a hand. "Simmer down. You're only fired for show. As far as Shaver's attorney knows, I've removed my team from consulting with Eddie. You'll still work it behind the scenes."

Mia's observant eyes catch my hard swallow. "You are worried."

"I'm not worried, Mia dear. I'm being cautious, as you said. Since Shaver is already focused on me, there's no reason to have that focus shift." I take a sip of water. "Just lay low until after my testimony, then we'll resume as usual."

Mia and Charlie seem uncertain, but they're not privilege to the interview or the tests. Shaver's scans came back and, even though there is some interesting activity going on in his ventromedial prefrontal cortex (that would be the part of the brain where we see general psychopath activity), his brain is otherwise trauma free.

There's no source to hang his temporary insanity hat on.

Of course, once I state this on the stand, declaring Shaver in control of his actions, his attorney will have a rebuttal witness to try to discredit me. That's fine. Eddie has the drug angle if we need to go there, but I know juries. This one will want to convict Shaver, they just need a narrative, and a believable, intelligent witness (that's me) to give them the okay.

Fear assuaged, conversation resumes around the booth. The restaurant buzzes with a low hum, a sort of mellow current. The atmosphere feels tranquil. Somewhere in my subconscious, a voice whispers, *the quiet before the storm*.

Then the storm herself walks in.

My chest catches fire at the sight of Porter.

A slim, black velvet dress hugs her curves, capping off just above the knee. Black stilettos lengthen her sexy legs. Her hair is loose and tumbles in waves over her bare shoulders.

She's sin incarnate.

As she spots our booth, a sly smile curves her pink lips. She heads our way, and I'm suddenly sweating. Heart palpitating. This feels like a test. Do I compliment her in front of the team, or wait until we're alone?

Then the thought of being alone with Porter stirs a visceral, carnal reaction in my groin. Damn, it's been too long.

I tamp down all these inappropriate thoughts as she slides in beside Mia. "Okay gang. Officially, I am not on this case with you."

"Technically, neither are we," Mia says.

Porter quirks an eyebrow, then directs her next words at me. "Ethically, I can't give you anything that the defense may use. But I can give you new information, and what you choose to do with that…" She slides a folder across the table.

I snag it and place the folder at my side. "Detective Renner came through?" I inquire.

Porter nods. "You already have everything on the crime scene, I assume, but Renner's investigation went beyond. She pulled phone records from as many of Shaver's associates as she could, and cross referenced those with Tillman's phone. Then she investigated Tillman's social media for the past year. Not easy to do amid a homicide investigation."

"What are you getting at?"

Porter leans over the table and lowers her voice. "You believed that stalking victims was a part of Shaver's MO, but had no way to prove it. Just a theory, right?"

I glance down at the file. "Porter, you're a goddess."

She smiles. "I know. Anyway, Renner is ready to take the stand to divulge what she's uncovered."

"Shaver has other victims," I say, thinking. But there are no bodies. His method changes with each kill, making it virtually impossible to link him to other murders. And yet, stalking… "We can look for the same stalking patterns."

Porter winks at me. "That's where Detective Renner was already heading. Just in case Shaver was acquitted."

It's just a flash, but I catch the down turn of her lips. Regret. Shame. She was on the wrong side, but she has nothing to feel bad about. Like she said, she was doing her job. I do understand that.

I begin to reach across the table, to take her hand, then remember we're not alone.

"Charlie, I need you to start cross referencing Shaver's *interests* with missing persons' cases." Interests being the women he was actively pursuing. Stalking in today's time doesn't mean you have to physically follow someone.

He nods assuredly. "First thing, Dr. West."

Mia and Porter are engaged in their own conversation, and I use the brief moment to really look at her. Suddenly, I can't look away. How have I gone three years without needing her input, her smile. Her comfort.

I remove the napkin from my lap. "Goodnight, all. I've taken care of the bill, so don't get carried away at the bar."

After a round of goodbyes, I make it to the door, where I pause and pretend to check my phone. Waiting for Porter, hoping she'll be right behind me. I spot her in my peripheral and push through to the outside.

She finds me around the corner. "That was abrupt."

"Because I couldn't wait to do this." I have her in my arms and kissing her, seeking her sweet lips like a parched man seeks water.

I am parched. I've been a shriveled shell of a man far too long. And I may be making the worst mistake with Porter, risking too much...but there's plenty of time for regret later. I know this all too well. Right now, I just want the feel of her pressed against me.

She breaks the kiss and finds my eyes. "My place?"

I can't talk, but I can nod like a bobble head, simultaneously shoving away every warning. Every fear. I latch on to the fiery ache in my chest, the heavy *thud* of my heart, the cues that signal to go with her. She takes my hand in hers and leads me across the street.

And here we are. We've come full circle.

Neuroplasticity.

My own brain's ability to grow and change.

I'm changing to be with Porter. My desire for her overrides the faulty wiring from the pain. Neurons are welded and new pathways formed. There's the fear—there's always the fear—that my pain will infect her, and I want to protect her from all the heartache and grief. But if I'm willing to betray a murderer, a madman, to protect her, then I can be strong enough to shield her from my shit, also.

I have to be.

The dark anguish within me won't reach her.

Believe the lie, my subconscious whispers. I hate that bastard.

Change starts small, then it grows. Rapidly. How all change happens. Three years ago I believed I could never love another woman again. Now, my brain (because the heart can't really feel emotions), is changing to allow the hope of *what if*.

What if I can move on? What if Porter is the one to mend all the broken and torn parts? What if I can let go of the pain?

My feelings for her won't be the same as my love for Mel, but we're built to *not want to do this alone*. Being alone is a choice. Just as taking a chance is. We are given an infinite way to love. I'm open to that.

The brain's ability to adapt to correct the damage is remarkable.

I'm ready.

10

KNIGHT OF SWORDS

DR. IAN WEST

With addiction, the mind picks up where it left off, like no time has passed since an alcoholic took that last drink, or an addict their last hit. The mind continues on a timeline, regardless of the amount of time sober between.

This is due to tolerance. Our tolerance continues to increase for a substance even when we're no longer feeding the craving. It's fascinating. At least it is to me, to think the mind never forgets; our habits, our desires—that are so deeply cemented in our psyche.

I'm thinking of this now as I sit on Porter's sofa, as I stare at her draped across the lounge directly in front of me, because my whole entire body craves her.

I pick up with Porter much in the same way, my body responding to her pheromones, to her laugh, her touch, yearning her, as if that night in the bar we *had* experienced that almost kiss.

"What are you thinking about?" she asks.

"Addiction," I blurt.

Her throaty laugh rolls over my skin, inviting. "Your mind never stops." She slides off the lounge and slinks toward the sofa, her walk slow, deliberate, a seduction. Her knees slide between mine. Tangible friction ignites my flesh. "Let me take your mind off…everything."

She reaches behind her back and begins to unzip her dress, the erotic sound driving my senses wild. I've seen Porter be sexy before. Every Halloween—Mel's favorite, remember?—Porter upped her game on the slutty costume contest.

I've witnessed her flirt with men. Watched her work her charm in the courtroom. I've seen this all just one place removed, never the target of her wiles.

And I admit, had she set her sights on me that first night…and Melanie never walked through that door…I'd have been just as helpless to resist her as I am now.

Her hand stops mid-zip, the top of her dress slouched low enough to reveal the swell of her breasts. I tear my gaze away from the tantalizing sight. "What's wrong?"

"Shit. I'm really nervous." Her laugh is forced, her voice wobbling with the effort.

A hollow twinge darts through my chest. I sit forward and clasp her hips, rest my forehead to the softness of her belly. The sigh that slithers free feels torn from my lungs. "It's okay. We can take it slow."

"I think three years is slow enough," she says. I feel her tremble, and I look up. "She won, you know. I did fight for you, that night after we left The Bar."

Confusion knits my brows together. "What?"

She exhales heavily. "I'm not a saint, West. And neither

was Mel, God love her pure soul." She zips up the dress and crosses her arms. "After we left the bar, much drunker than we needed to be, it started out as a joke. Maybe we could share you. Then Mel made a comment like, "may the best woman win". Then we got into it. Saying things in our drunken state that we both regretted, that nearly cost us our future friendship. When I sobered up, I realized how stupid I'd been." She shakes her head. "There was never any contest. There was no denying your feelings for her. You chose her the moment you laid eyes on her, and I had to make a choice."

I swallow. She chose to hide her feelings for me. For Mel. "You cared about her more."

"Well, yeah." She smiles, and it's beautiful. "I mean, not that you weren't a great catch back then, enough to make two drunken girls lose their mind for a night." She winks. "But you weren't the only man in DC. And Mel was already becoming someone special to me. It's damn hard to find a good friend."

I take her hands and slide them down her hips, then I ease off the sofa. I stand so close to her I can inhale her lavender. Feel the press of her body heat against my suit. I hook a finger beneath her chin and tip her head back. "You are a saint. And you have enough space in your saint heart for both of us."

Her swallow pulses against my finger. "So do you."

I kiss her, my lips tentative at first, waiting for her to match me. Then I deepen the kiss, parting her lips against mine. Breathing her in. It's a slow burn kiss. The kind that kindles a flame, then the embers smolder into an inferno.

I caress her curves, hands mapping her body over the velvet dress, then they amble their way to her back, where I find that infuriating zipper. I lower it, my fingertips tracing her skin as I drag the dress down along her body, and she allows it to slip to the floor.

This should feel off, or strange at first. Making out with Porter. But my body responds to her touch, her taste, as if it's unfurling a recorded memory. Maybe from another life, or alternate universe. Where Porter and I never had any barriers between us.

Her hands snake up to my shoulders and she pushes me down on the couch. It's the most erotic sight watching her spread her legs to straddle me. Then the feel of her on my lap...

I ease out a hiss. "Be gentle," I warn. "It's been a minute." *Way longer...*

Her hair creates a veil around us, the dim light of candles setting her amber highlights aglow, ethereal. A sinful angel sent to wreck me.

"West, that's the very reason to be anything but gentle." She clasps the front of my pants and works the button with maddening leisure.

Not to sound crass, but I've been rock-hard since she asked me to her apartment. I'm one pulsating vein at this point, and every time her fingers skim my boxers, my dick jumps, excited for attention.

Then she circles me fully, the feel of her soft hand stroking me sends me careening over the edge. Control lost.

I bury my hand in her hair and bring her mouth to mine. A crash of senses, overwhelming. My throttle just snapped. I have her bra off with a deftness I'm impressed I still obtain. I kiss a heated trail down her neck, sucking at her silky skin, until my mouth skims her nipple. I swirl my tongue around one, then the other, desperate to give each equal attention.

Her heavy breaths ease beneath my skin, igniting my flesh. Her fingers play at the back of my neck. Christ, I'm on fire. I palm her ass and haul her up against my chest before I lay her flat against the sofa. I tear my suit jacket off and toss it.

Porter's breathless laugh infuses me as she works my tie loose. "Come here," she commands, and oh, I obey.

I cover her body with mine, falling into her. Consumed. She snaps the buttons of my dress shirt open, tugging it off my shoulders, both of us in a heated frenzy to remove every barrier. As her silk-soft skin caresses mine, our bodies molding into one, a sense of seamless completeness washes through me.

Her nails drag over my back, her teeth nibble at my earlobe, eliciting a desperate need to ravish every inch of her. My fingers seek the apex between her thighs, and I stroke her soft panties, driving myself mad at the wet, smooth feel of her.

"Christ," I breathe, as I come undone. I want her so badly…just put me out of my misery.

She bucks against my hand, undulating her hips to place me where she wants, and it drives me fucking crazy. "I want you inside me. Now, West."

For once, I don't think. I'm a man of action. All the fear and trepidation falls away as I slip her panties down and, as I slide my hand beneath her hips, lift her up to meet me. A hard shiver racks my muscles as I tense at the feel of her.

She does this thing with her hips that pushes me deeper, and I curse. "Fuck. Are you trying to kill me?"

Her hands go to my hair, fingers splaying and gripping, as she rolls her hips. "I've stored up a lot of fantasies… This might take all night."

Jesus. I bury my face in her neck and thrust inside her, deeper. Harder. My dick already throbbing with the pressure to release.

"You feel too good..." Dammit. I have no control. I cup her shoulders as she arches against me, her perfect fucking tits sensually rubbing my chest with every hungry thrust.

We become a wrapped pretzel on the couch, her legs locking mine, and I can't get enough. I rock into her until I'm a fucking machine, then I have to kiss her just to ease the building desire to fuck her right into the couch.

She kisses me back, our tongues probing and just as desperate to take as our bodies. Breaths labored, she turns her head to whisper against my ear. "Don't hold back." Her words are a tease against my skin, daring me.

Madness; that's what it feels like. When raw, unadulterated desire overtakes your senses, and you become a slave to it. I have no will of my own. I take her body, frantically craving every throaty moan, every cry of pleasure, until I feel her clench—so fucking tight, I shatter—and she breaks around me.

I collapse, loving the feel of her heavy breaths that fan my face. Her chest heaves in sync with mine, the roar of my heart fading as I come down, sated.

She brushes her fingers through my hair, and I kiss her neck. "We can do that another hundred times...then you might be close to making it up to me."

A laugh barrels free. "So your revenge is death by sex." But I kiss her, slow and tender. And I will spend my every waking moment making the last three years up to her.

THE DEAD TALKS

DR. IAN WEST

I feel reborn. I'm the same man, but I've been picked up and dusted off. Buffed and shined. Baptized in the church of Porter.

Melodramatic? Maybe a little. But it's not just the sex (which was mind-blowing, BTW); it's having taken the next, frightening step, and not fallen on my ass in epic failure.

I'm a psychologist, if you recall, and I'm well aware that three years is an unhealthy length of time to be celibate after the loss of a partner. If you also recall, I dislike general psychology. Hence why you don't see me in a big, comfy chair asking neurotics how they feel.

Given that the grieving process is different for everyone, I came to accept the long-er journey for myself. Fuck Kübler-Ross' five stages. *I did it my way!* Sung in the Sid Vicious version (not Sinatra). Sarcasm and Netflix kept me company when I wasn't consumed with work.

Work is an excellent way to avoid.

I'm at the sink in the men's courthouse lavatory, admiring the healthy color of my skin, the way my gray suit hangs just right today. I wash my hands and smooth the top of my hair down before I leave.

I'm like a giddy kid on his first day of school, except it's better. It's the first day of court. A brand new case. Clean slate.

Sort of.

"I'm heading in," I tell Mia. "Did you get the background check on juror number seven?"

"Charlie got it. Our history teacher doesn't vote. No trail on him."

"All right." I'll need to evaluate him in person, then. See if I can get a vibe. Juror number seven, Andrew Smith, is our question mark juror. His answers were what we wanted to hear during *voir dire*, but I'm not sure which way he's swaying.

The mock jury was skewed because of this one juror. I can't have that happen during the actual trial.

I push through the courtroom doors, a flutter in my stomach as I look to see where Porter is seated. She's benched for another week at her firm, but this is a high-profile case. Her firm will still want her to follow it closely.

Only she hasn't made it yet.

I take my usual seat in the middle of the fifth row and dig out my phone. I type out a short text to her, then stall, thumbs hovering over the screen. That brand new court smell isn't the only thing working on my nerves.

I finish out the text, keeping it simple: *Saved you a spot.*

No mushy, lovey dovey shit. Porter knows me better than that. I don't have to force it with her, just as we didn't have to force our friendship. I can still be the same man, and that's a relief.

Besides, Porter hates that crap. And thank fuck for that.

We didn't discuss what happens next. We didn't have the after sex relationship talk. We don't have to. We took the step. We're here. It just is. And it feels right.

The bailiff walks by my row and coughs. Loudly. I glance over to catch his narrowed gaze on my phone. I mouth a lame apology and shut the phone down.

"Someone is extra peppy and forgetful today," Mia chimes in my ear. "So unlike you, Dr. West. What gives?"

The way she says it, as if she already suspects the answer, has me yanking my collar away from my neck. Someone just turned up the heat. "None of your business, Mia." It has to be stated, because it's useless to lie to an analyst when she's worked for you long enough to know your tells down to a science. Behavioral science, that is.

"Porter looked beautiful last night," she says, fishing, dangling the bait. "Don't you think?"

See? There are no secrets in my company. "Yes, she did. That dress was very becoming on her. Now get back to work."

Her giggle echoes over the line. "Yes, sir."

I'm smiling. I can't help it. I'd forgotten what carefree felt like. How light it makes your head, as if you're drugged. I go to check my phone for Porter's reply and remember it's off.

I glance at my watch, then the doors.

The bailiff declares court in session and announces the judge. O'Hare is the presiding judge, and I thank my lucky stars. "Judge O'Hare loves me," I whisper to Mia.

Her *pfft* makes my statement a little less believable. "Remember when he threw you out of court?"

Right. That. "He's like…a thousand years old. He can't possibly remember that."

Judge O'Hare squints in my direction, his mouth drawn in a thin line. Well damn.

"Let's just focus on the jury," I tell Mia. "They're what matters."

"I've updated their profiles. Ready to go," she confirms.

I crack my knuckles.

The feel of being watched prickles my skin, and I look toward the defense table. Shaver is fixated on me, a shrewd glint in his eyes. No smile today. He's focused, determined. A business man. His lips move, but I don't catch what he's saying. At his slight nod, I look away.

After Shaver delivers his plea, the trial commences, and Smigel doesn't pussyfoot around. In his opening statement, he goes right for the insanity trifecta. Brain damage, psychotic state, and recovered memories.

The jury is reactive. That's fine. They're a sponge right now; fresh and primed to absorb information. Once this trial drags on, and they become weary of testimonies and scientific jargon, that's when you hit them with the shock and awe. Revive them. Bring them back to life.

And nail Shaver where it hurts.

The truth.

I've heard Eddie's opening statement twice now, and it still gives me chills. He hammers down the facts, what the prosecution is going to prove. That Shaver suffered no brain damage. That the notorious drug lord who has evaded arrest over the years is intelligent and manipulative—that he's going to try to deceive the jury with his practiced mannerisms. But that Quentin Shaver is a psychopathic predator who deliberately and methodically stalked Devin

Tillman, abducted her, then tortured and killed and mutilated his victim.

Eddie calls the first witness, Dr. Maxine Prentice. The medical examiner who examined Devin Tillman.

Yeah. We're not pussyfooting around, either.

If Smigel wants to prove Shaver was in a temporary state of psychosis when he murdered Tillman, then he has to prove haste. The very word *temporary* denotes a hurried act. It's true a delusion can last days, even months or years, but there's no fugue state at play here. There's a *snapped* defense, which claims Shaver was outside himself during this hastened episode where he killed the victim.

Dr. Prentice recites her credentials, then Eddie asks the ME to divulge her findings during the examination.

"I discovered contusions located around the victim's wrists and ankles that were already in the stages of healing. The abrading on the skin led me to believe she had been bound for hours before her death."

Eddie looks at the jury as he asks, "Such as bound by rope?"

The ME nods. "Yes. Rope is the most likely cause for this type of abrading and bruising. The ligature marks on the victim's wrists measured out to be comparable to most commonly used cotton rope. The victim also suffered from dehydration, as determined by her skin tissue and organs."

Confirming the prosecution's theory of stalking and torturing the victim is the DA's office's main goal. That can lead to a broader investigation into other missing persons to locate more potential victims of Shaver.

"What about the torture and murder itself? Can you tell us, in your professional opinion, how long the perpetrator tortured Devin Tillman before she was brutally stabbed to death?"

"Objection, Your Honor." Smigel stands. "Speculation. Despite the expert's credentials, she can't definitively know the timeline."

Judge O'Hare shrugs. "Well, I'd like to hear her answer, then decide if it's credible. Overruled. Please answer the question, Dr. Prentice."

Judge O'Hare wins the day. "I like him. Why did he throw me out again?" I ask Mia.

"You argued with him about one of his rulings."

Oh. Well, that will do it.

The ME goes into detail about the science, which I fear is getting lost on the jury. We did well in selecting practical, intelligent jurors, but even my eyelids are starting to feel heavy.

Eddie presses the doctor to explain in layman's terms. Good for him.

"If we look at time of death, we can count backward, using the layers of congealed blood like measures of time, like on the rings of a tree. The victim was bound and unable to defend herself. According to my blood analysis report, I deduced the victim was tortured for nine hours before she ultimately died due to hypoxia via exsanguination. The femoral artery was stabbed and severed." She glances at the jury and amends. "She bled out."

"So despite the mutilation to the torso, the fatal wound was not delivered to the victim's heart, doctor?" Eddie clicks the remote in his hand, and an image of Tillman's corpse discovered at the crime scene appears on the flatscreen.

The jury reacts. Five cover their mouths, two look away, and my question mark juror tilts his head. Appall rolls through them all in different stages. This is why Eddie chose this question, so he could show the image. It's harsh, but so is the crime. The jury needs to experience what Shaver did to this woman.

I glance at the screen, even though I've stared at the crime scene photos too many times now. Before I look back at the jury, something nags at the back of my mind. The familiarity of the crime scene—but not because I've studied it. Tillman's torso is bound with rope. A black blindfold covers her eyes.

Shit.

The severe mutilation of the body never allowed me to see past the gore. I admit, I chose not to practice in the medical field for a reason. I don't do blood and death.

But I see it now.

"Mia," I mutter. "Pull up the Eight of Swords Tarot card."

"Okay..."

"What does it look like?"

"Eight swords surround a woman who's bound with rope and blindfolded—" I hear it in her pause. Mia makes the connection.

"Eight stab wounds," I say, putting it together. "Tillman's card was the Eight of Swords. Find out everything you can about that card. It's meaning, history. Everything. Get Charlie on investigating anything that card has to do between Tillman and Shaver."

"On it, Dr. West."

Got you, fucker. Shaver's MO. He doesn't just use the Tarot for victim selection; he stages the scene. It's part of his ritual. He doesn't have to leave a card behind, because the whole scene is a damn tarot card. If we have to search every card in the Arcana to compare it to every gory crime scene across every state... We'll find his victims.

I tuned out, and now the ME is wrapping up her testimony.

"The victim was already dead when the perpetrator removed the heart. My blood analysis report also states this," Dr. Prentice says.

Shaver's lawyer will try to use this to further his client's claim of a delusional state. I recall Shaver's reference to holding Tillman's still-beating heart in his hand. He's planned this all out. Down to the ME's report.

"Thank you, Dr. Prentice," Eddie says. "I have no further questions for this witness, Your Honor."

Smigel stands to start his cross examination, but the judge calls a recess. "We'll resume after lunch."

I give Eddie a nod of approval on his expert questioning, and then file into line. I have my phone in hand before I'm out of the courtroom. Once it's powered on, I wait for the beep to alert me of Porter's reply message.

I need her to know this. She might have more information —something we could use to help Eddie nail Shaver for good.

My damn phone remains silent.

I open the text app anyway. When I don't see a text from her, I move farther down the hallway for privacy and call her number. It goes to voicemail.

Do you ever get those moments where your existence seems to suspend?

Where your heart slows but fires like a cannon. Sounds and movements blur and feel muted; the roar of the ocean in your head. Time just stops.

This moment seizes me now.

It's the moment of confirmation that something is wrong

—that something bad has happened. But you can't accept it yet.

Phone in hand, I stare at the screen, my breathing coming too loudly in my ears. Mia's voice sounds over the line, and I remove the earbud.

Then I hear Eddie trying to gain my attention.

I look up. "I have to go."

He blinks, stunned. "Right now? We're about to resume court."

"You got this. You know what to do." I pat his shoulder as I head around him.

"Dr. West…? Ian, wait—" He trails after me.

He never calls me that, and for this reason, I respond. "I can't. I have to go. Just focus on the case."

The desperate edge in my tone makes him halt at the end of the hallway. "You got it. Good luck."

Luck. That damn Tarot card in my pocket suddenly comes to mind, because—I realize—that's what Shaver mouthed in court today. That's what I couldn't make out.

Good luck.

I hurry through the metal detector and out to the courthouse steps.

I keep dialing Porter's number as I race to her apartment.

FIRST CUP

DR. IAN WEST

The landlord of Porter's building will not open her door. I'm seconds away from pushing him aside and ramming my body against the damn thing when he says, "Sir, if you make a report to the police—"

"No. They can't help me." I drive a hand through my hair, furious. "Look. I'm a personal friend of Ms. Lovell's. I was just here with her last night. Check your security footage. She might be in there, hurt. She might need medical attention."

His eyes narrow into suspicious slits. "Did you do something to her?"

In a flash, anger ignites my blood. My muscles act of their own accord. I have him by the collar and jacked up against the wall. "Like I'm about to do to you?"

I snatch the key ring from his belt and dangle it in front of his face. "Don't ever say that. Ever. I'm going in there now. Call the cops if you want. But I guarantee this building is probably in violation of at least three codes that I'll spot on my way down in handcuffs. And me and the DA's office are like this." I cross my fingers.

"Let go of me." He yanks free, and I let him. He's winded, taking deep breaths, and he hasn't even started to run yet. "There are no tapes. Cameras are for show, so I don't give a fuck. Go on."

Good to know Porter's landlord is a selfish pig. As he heads down the hallway, I insert the key slowly and turn the deadlock, listening out for any strange sounds as I ease the door open.

My heart vaults into my throat. I'm trying not to think about Porter scared. Hurt. Or worse—but these thoughts invade my mind, relentless. Worry and dread—that fucking dread—ratchet my adrenaline until I can't control the tremble taking over.

The apartment is quiet. It appears the same as I left it this morning, with Porter still asleep, curled beneath the covers. I kissed her on the forehead without waking her, then made my exit, locking the door on my way out.

The note I placed on the bar is still there. Untouched.

I head to the bedroom. The bed is made. As I turn the corner to check the bathroom, something odd catches my notice.

On the mantel are five cups.

Goblets, more specifically. Sterling silver, and they look vintage. Expensive. My heart thunders, pulse rioting against my veins. I take a step toward the cups, then stop.

Shaver stages his scenes.

Fuck. My hand tears at my hair. Fuck. Fuck. *Fuck.*

I close my eyes, willing my brain to think, to rationalize. The cups placed here is a message from Shaver. Just like the

Tarot card. And just like Mel's gravesite, someone has been inside Porter's apartment.

Mind on overdrive, I tear through her room, tossing covers and lifting the bed. I check underneath, then the bathroom. I hunt every room, looking for a clue, evidence. Anything to show me where she could be.

Then I open the closet.

The dresses and suits have been pushed aside, and deeply grooved footprints mark the carpeted area. As if someone stood here for hours…

Watching us.

I whirl around and stare at the bed.

Christ. One of his cronies was in the fucking apartment with us while we were making love. Then I left this morning…leaving her alone with some twisted fuck.

Now she's gone.

I pull out my phone and search my contacts. I need someone I can trust—someone who has connections, who can bypass procedures. I start to call Charlie. His father retired from the force last year; he's experienced and still has an inside beat. But dammit, I need someone that will believe Shaver is behind this—and who won't think twice about operating outside the law.

Someone that knows how to handle an abduction.

That word hits me like a punch to the gut. I topple over, hands to knees, dragging air into my constricted lungs.

Cold sweat blankets my forehead. I wipe at my face, still trying to process what this all means. I glance at the silver cups lined up on the mantel. It's a message, but the answer isn't there. It's with Shaver.

I poke the earbud in my ear. "Mia, are you there?"

"Where have you been? Eddie is like, really concerned, Dr. West."

"Listen. I need you to do something. And I need it done right now."

Her affirmation comes a second too slow "All right."

I look around the room, then decide this isn't the place to discuss strategies. I leave the apartment, making sure to bolt the door, then pocket the key as I jog to the elevator. Once inside, I pull the red button, and the car jerks to a halt.

"I need you to set off the fire alarm at the courthouse," I tell her.

Her laugh sounds frantic. "Are you drunk?"

"No." I search the elevator quickly, deciding it's safe. "Porter's missing. It's Shaver."

"Oh, god..." I hear clicking over the line. "How do you know—?"

"There's no time, Mia. Just trust me. It's Shaver, and Porter is gone. We need to get Shaver out of court where I can access him. I need to talk to him."

"Okay. I'm on it. I always knew there'd be a day when you'd give me a reason to use my hacking skills. I just can't believe..."

"I know. We'll find her. That piece of shit isn't going to hurt her. He's just..." A thought hits me.

I whip out the Tarot card I keep in my pocket. The Five of Cups. I read the fucking card wrong. It wasn't about me...about my loss, my grief. Mia was right. It's about what I can still lose.

Porter.

"She's alive," I say, relief suddenly washing over me.

Mia's silence thickens my throat. "How do you know?" Her voice wavers.

I stare at the card. "Because for Shaver to get what he wants, she has to be."

"The alarm is enabled," Mia announces. She's been working on it since I left Porter's building. "I'm a little rusty, it seems. But I did it. Is there anything else I can do to help?"

I'm standing on the courthouse steps when the fire alarm sounds. Seconds later, people file out through the doors. "Keep this quiet for now. Charlie can't know yet."

"Right. His dad. We're not getting the police involved?"

"Not yet. I'm on my way inside. Just hang tight until I call you. And…thank you, Mia." I disconnect the line and remove the earpiece. Then I make sure to pocket the transmitter I keep on my tie. Just in case Mia gets too curious and tries to listen in.

I weave a path toward the doors through the press of anxious people loitering on the steps. Court officers have set up post at the doors, restricting anyone from entering. Shit. I didn't think about that.

Heading around the side, I spot a few stragglers exiting through an emergency door. I run. "Hold the door—" I catch the Exit door before it closes.

"There's a fire—"

"I know. Thanks." I ignore the lady's baffled look as I go in and close the door behind me.

The guards aren't going to evacuate Shaver unless there's proof of danger. Even then, there are protocols that take a lengthy amount of time to have him removed from the building.

The elevators have been shut down, so I dash up the first flight of stairs, rage fueling every frantic step.

The courthouse holding cells are—thank God—on the second level. I hear guards shuffling prisoners to the cells, and I duck behind a corner where I call Eddie.

"Meet me at the holding cells. I need you to get me access to Shaver."

"What the hell, Ian?"

I blow out a breath, exasperated. "Questions later. Do you trust me?"

"You know I do."

"Then get your rich, ADA ass up here and get me inside a room with Shaver." I end the call and phone Mia. "You can disable the alarm now. I think court has been adequately delayed."

"You got it, Dr. West. Please, keep me updated."

Impatient, I pace the hall. Strip off my suit jacket. I'm just about to force my way to Shaver when Eddie rounds the corner.

I jump straight in. "Shaver's done something with Porter. She's missing. There's evidence at her apartment that could prove he had her taken. So I need to be in a room with him. Now. And I need privacy."

A wave of shock crashes across Eddie's face, his expression morphing from annoyed to stricken. "Are you sure?"

Disbelief is always our go-to reaction when faced with tragedy. I've had unfortunate experience, so my effort to work past my own denial for Porter's sake wastes no time. But I still feel like we're wasting a shit-ton right now.

"Yes. Eddie, I need this. Make it happen."

He nods, the reality and urgency of the situation settling

over him like a frigid current. "Fucking hell. That fucking sick bastard."

As I move toward holding, he makes a call to Smigel. Shaver's troll attorney. "Want to chat about a deal?"

I raise an eyebrow. That's one way to get Smigel's attention.

"Your expert witness, Dr. West, requests a confidential meeting with Shaver," Eddie continues.

Outside holding, I let them work out the logistics while I roll up my sleeves. Every nerve in my body is jumping with anticipation. Sweat drips down the middle of my back. The musty smell of the courthouse twists my stomach.

"All right," Eddie says, as he approaches. "Twenty minutes. Smigel thinks I have a deal to offer, so he's willing to hear me out and let you talk with Shaver while court is still postponed."

As the guards head our way, I ask, "Can you lead him on that long?"

"Please. I work in the DA's office." He ducks his head to whisper, "Hang that bastard if you have to. I've got your back." Then he tells the guards they're required to wait outside the door for our confidential meeting.

I'm escorted into holding by two guards, and when I glimpse Shaver seated in the consultation room, it takes every bit of my willpower not to leap over the table.

The door is locked behind me. The guards take up post on the other side. It's just me and Shaver.

"Dr. West. Finally. You've come for your reading."

13

HANGMAN

DR. IAN WEST

"Where is she?"

"She's safe, Dr. West."

I palm the edge of the table to hold myself upright. It's not relief; I'm well aware that Shaver could be lying, that he's an expert in manipulation, especially with his practiced, conveyed emotions.

No, it's desperation. I'm desperate to believe him, regardless of it all.

"Now, your reading—"

"Fuck your reading. I want to know *where* Porter is." Strength renewed, I look into his eyes, unyielding.

Unaffected, Shaver tilts his head, more curious about my reactive state. "Don't you want to know *why*, Dr. West? That would be the more logical question in order to obtain the object of your desire more promptly."

My knuckles turn white against the dark trim. "I don't have to ask."

"Ah. That's right. You read people. You already have the answer. Shame you didn't figure it out sooner, though."

I round the table and barrel toward Shaver, getting close enough to smash his face. My fists ache, clenched tightly at my sides, as I restrain from doing just that.

Shaver's lips tip into a devious smile. "I envy your emotions," he says. "How does that anger feel?"

Teeth gritted, heart thundering, I force myself to move back. The maddening truth is that Shaver wants control, and by losing mine, I'm serving him all the power.

"Very impressive," he says, his accent grating my already frayed nerves. "So let's press on. There's something important I need to know before we can…help one another."

My eyes seal closed. I count to three before I open them, centered. "What?"

"How do you see your cup, Dr. West? Half full, or half empty? Her life depends on your answer."

It takes my last well of restraint not to end him right here. "She's not a part of this."

He doesn't waver. No fear that I'll make good on my macho display. "Of course she is. She's been the center of it from the start. Now, have a seat, Dr. West." He turns to face the table. "We don't have long, and there are rules you need to understand."

The thing about psychopaths: they have to feel in control.

Every fiber of my being revolts against giving Shaver what he wants, but for Porter, to know that she's safe… I take a step back. Then take another step away. I unclench my hands, allow blood flow to temper my anger and murderous thoughts.

I want to drag him over the table and beat the answer out; nothing would give me greater pleasure than causing him physical pain. But I seat myself across from him and breathe slowly, evenly. "You had Porter taken to ensure my testimony."

"Insurance in this matter is utmost important," he says. "Why else would you take the stand and testify to my being insane?"

Of course, I asked myself this very thing. I weighed Shaver's egotistical nature with the fact that he does suffer antisocial pathologies. I'm out of practice in dealing with patients on a one-on-one basis. I recognized the threat, yet in my own vain way, I assumed it was solely directed toward me, and not anyone else.

Porter is an extension of me. Shaver saw this. She is his bartering chip.

"You testify in three days," Shaver continues. "Once you complete your task, I'll have proof that Porter is well and alive delivered to you."

"No. I want that now, and once I testify, I want her released."

He *tsks*. "I can't do that, Dr. West. See, you could just as easily retract your testimony. The case needs to be over, the jury ruling in my favor. Then your world will be made right again."

Bargaining with a madman is a practice in idiocy. And it's dangerous. This won't end well. He's smart enough to know that I can retract my statement at any time. Either before or after the trial. Inciting unethical practices (extremely) on his and his attorney's part. With proof of Porter's abduction, a whole lot of damage would follow.

He has no plans to set Porter free.

That's not his MO. Before Tillman, there were no bodies.

My thoughts fight not to go there, but I know it in my bones. Porter will never be seen again. Her body never found.

I'm slipping into a dark place with this realization. I school my features not to show just how terrified I am. This might be my only chance to glean information from him—information that can save Porter.

"Three days," I say, my voice raw. "Then why five cups, Shaver? You're a methodical man. That just doesn't line up."

His gaze tics over my face, searching for my angle. "The Five of Cups has always haunted me," he says. "But it never appeared in any of my readings until the first day of the trial. The gypsy said the cloaked man would be my salvation, and there you were. Cloaked in your shroud of grief. And there Porter was, your full, overflowing cup." He shakes his head. "So much history, so much waste."

"You'd be a fool not to exploit it," I supply.

He shrugs, unapologetic. "I don't want to go to prison." He straightens his suit leisurely, as if he's not on trial for murder.

"You could choose not to kill and mutilate women," I say, mocking. "That's always a good insurance policy."

"You hide behind sarcasm. That must get exhausting. Here's the truth, Dr. West: It is immaterial to me whether I behave well or ill, for virtue itself is no security." A beat. "Do you know what that means?"

An annoyed scoff. "I know that quote doesn't belong anywhere near you."

"No, it belongs to the people, and it's a testament to the savageness of our poorly executed justice system. What John Adams stated is a truth so deeply ingrained in our culture, every last citizen fears the police and court. We are not innocent until proven guilty. You above all should know this.

You're a trial consultant. You're a part of the corrupt practice of this institution. You select juries to assure wins for your clients. Your colleagues violate privacy, and expose secrets." He sits forward. "And you assume to judge me. Who is really in the wrong?"

We have left reality. "I don't care about your opinions. I don't care about your absurd justifications, or butchering of quotes. Answer the fucking question." *You sick, demented bastard.*

"You didn't look inside the cups, did you? Because if you had, we'd be having a very different conversation right now."

My blood ices. My eyes close as I force the words out. "What's in the cups?"

I'm out of my depth. I have to find a way to bury my emotions. Emotive reaction won't result in getting Porter back. My fear is his nectar of life.

"Did you know that blood doesn't evaporate?" he asks. His gaze lingers on my face, analyzing me. "You have to add an anticoagulant, and you have to use a precise mixture to use evaporation as a timer. Very old-school, but then I enjoy a more vintage approach."

It hits me with a sick dread. Porter's blood…

My voice is low, guttural. "Her blood? Her fucking blood is in those cups? What did you do to her?"

All attempts at controlling emotions are officially the fuck gone.

"Nothing compared to what I'm going to – oh, so – enjoy doing to her if you try to cross me in any way, Dr. West."

Fuck it. I push the table. Hard. I remove the obstacle between me and the psycho. I'm in front of Shaver and peering down at him, mind lost. My fist makes contact with his face. Pain webs through my knuckles. But I grab his collar and strike again. I keep pounding, the smack of wet blood fueling my fire, until the pain numbs.

Hands are on me. I'm ripped away. My back hits the wall. One of the guards locks his forearm across my chest as I struggle, mindless, to get at Shaver.

In the chaos, Eddie arrives and convinces the guard to release me, but the cuffs go on. "Is that necessary?" Eddie demands.

The officer stares at my blood-stained hands and says, "It's not that I haven't wanted to do that very thing, Dr. West. But I'm sorry. I have to put you in holding."

"Dammit." Eddie scrubs his hands down his face. "All right. Just hang tight. Let me work it out."

There's nothing to work out. I glance at Shaver, bruised, blood streaming from his nose and mouth, and know that I've officially sentenced Porter to death. I'll be locked away. I'll be removed as an expert witness from the trial.

Chest heaving, I nearly crumple to the floor. "I tried," I hear myself say. And I did try to contain the rage—but it's been an active, simmering volcano for three years. On the cusp and ready to blow.

For months after Mel died, I envisioned hunting down that driver and beating him to a bloody pulp, then running him down with a car. I became fixated on that idea of justice. And now, all I can say is that, when faced with an actual villain—one where I can deliver punishment myself—the top blew.

Years of suppressed violence roared to the surface.

Shaver became the center of evil in the world that keeps taking and taking.

As the officer escorts me out of the room, I find and hold Shaver's eyes.

"Revenge feels good, doesn't it?" Shaver tries to bait me. "You have a pocket full of righteousness, Dr. West."

"Don't respond to that," Eddie counsels. He's already acting as my attorney.

Yeah. I'm going to need a good one.

Inside holding, I have time to think.

Too much time.

Which, admittedly, we don't get enough of that pure solitude in life. Where every electronic is removed, out of reach. When all we have is the quiet, and time. And thoughts.

I relive the past few hours in a haze. Porter's apartment. Shaver. Seeing myself over him. Blood. I bury my head in my bruised hands, going over it again. The cups—five cups. Shaver has a purpose for me, and it's bigger than getting him acquitted on an insanity defense.

I know this, because he told me a story about a gypsy and a Tarot card. Which I have no idea if it was even true, but he's fixated on this card and it's meaning. It's vital to him; so there has to be something I'm not seeing.

I laugh, a mocking, self-loathing laugh that encapsulates my uselessness. I haven't seen Shaver coming from day one. My arrogance made sure of that.

I go over the events again, fingers gripped in my hair, willing the answer from my fucking skull. *A pocket full of righteousness.*

What the hell does that mean...?

I stand up and pat my slacks, then check my jacket. A ribbon of hope curls through my apprehension as I pull a slip of paper from my inseam pocket. As I unfold it, I realize

Shaver's baiting was more than just to get a reaction. He needed me to get close enough.

To the cloaked man of the Five of Cups.

He should be wary of trusting fools. The system he's invested in has already betrayed and failed him once. He sees only what is lost. For this reason, his mourning will never end, even when a shiny new cup has been presented to him. In order to accept this new vessel, he must follow the path that sets his adversary free, forsaking his principles. Blood was spilt for his consuming grief. A sacrifice made for his future. A love that will heal. He will either take the new journey, embrace it and drink to prosperity—or the rest of her blood will spill.

PS - Three days. Three cups that will run dry. You've already lost so much, Dr. West. Don't waste the last two.

Son of a bitch. I ball the note and pitch it at the cement wall. My body sags against the bench. My knuckles throb from every punch delivered to that sadistic bastard, and it feels good.

Shaver delivered a Tarot reading to me, after all. He's won every round. I could spend hours analyzing his words, getting inside his head…but the only thing I can focus on is Porter. If I don't take the stand and declare him insane—god—he will bleed her.

So fine. I swear on the Bible and stand before the court and announce he's innocent of murdering Devin Tillman.

What then? At the end of the trial, Porter is suddenly set free? All evidence of her abduction wiped clean? Hardly. Shaver made a reference to how good revenge feels… knowing damn well that I'll deliver that vengeance to him in a heartbeat.

A *clang* rebounds around the cell, and footfalls sound,

coming closer. The officer who locked me inside opens the door. "You're free to go."

Eddie stands on the other side, hands tucked into his pockets. He looks weary. By the time I get my items back from holding, I'm feeling the same way.

Once outside, the fresh fall air hits my face. I inhale deeply, cleansing my lungs of the musty courthouse jail. "How did you spring me?"

Eddie guides me toward his BMW. "I made a deal with a devil."

"Oh. You too?"

He whirls around, features rimmed in anger. "This isn't a joke, Ian. You had Mia hack the courthouse security system and initiate the fire alarm to get Shaver out of court. Porter has been taken…and we don't even know by whom, or what is happening to her. You punched a man amid his trial in the fucking courthouse." He turns away, walks a few feet, then comes back at me. Finger pointed in my face. "I'm taking you to your office and then I'm getting my ass back in court. Can I trust you not to break any more laws today?"

Damn. When did Edward Vince Wagner grow a set. "You think I care about laws right now? What should I do? Call the cops? What do you think the police will do?" I step in front of his car door to block him. "What, Eddie? They won't even declare her missing until the twenty-four hour mark, and by then…"

I can't finish my thought. I don't know what tomorrow holds for Porter, and that makes me feel so damn helpless my chest tightens.

He releases an exasperated sigh. Drives a hand through his hair that is already disheveled, as if he's been repeating that action for the past hour. "After the trial is adjourned today, I'll help. I'll do what I can. But I can't be a part of anything illegal."

My head snaps back. As a lawyer in the DA's office, I get where he's coming from. But what I don't get is how he can be so cavalier about Porter—about not doing everything in our power to find her.

"How did you get me out?" I demand this time.

His gaze drops to the asphalt. "It was Shaver."

"What do you mean?"

"He told Smigel that he fell down a flight of stairs during the evacuation. I paid off the two guards to go along with his story. Shaver didn't look too bad once he was cleaned up." He shrugs. "Happens more than you think."

"Falling down stairs, or defendants getting the shit beat out of them?"

He glares at me. "Payoffs."

Yes. It does happen. But not to Eddie. He's a walk-the-line prosecutor. He's never had to manipulate the system… until today. For me. "I owe you one."

He huffs derisively. "Damn straight you do. But just…" He trails off, finally looking me in the eyes. "I care about Porter, too. I don't want to see her hurt. I know you don't trust authorities." He frowns. "But getting them involved is your best bet if someone has taken her, Ian. That's my two cents."

I nod to appease him, but Eddie doesn't know the details yet. There's more to weigh here than just the black and white. When the cops fail to find her, just like they failed to find Mel's hit-and-run driver, then Shaver will make me pay.

And Porter will suffer for my failure.

"All this is so wrong," he says, shaking his head. "You need to be cautious. Shaver isn't playing with a full deck."

I blink. A realization dawning. "What did you just say?"

"I'm saying, this is going to blow up in all our faces—"

"No, you said Shaver's not playing with a full deck." I walk around his car and open the passenger-side door. "Let's go."

Shaver isn't insane. He's intelligent and meticulous, and he's definitely playing with a full deck—a deck of Tarot cards.

14

LAND OF THE LOST

DR. IAN WEST

My sixth-floor office space has been converted to a headquarters.

Luckily, the open-floor plan made this transition easy. I put Charlie in charge of investigating Shaver's background. Any link, any clue, any connection that could lead us to Porter's trail goes up on the board.

The giant murder board Mia and Charlie were creating has been removed, set aside to contend with later. *After*. Once Porter is safe.

I have Mia focused on the jury. She's my only analyst, and I need her smart brain reading the jury during the trial. If we fail—and we will not; cannot—our only hope remains with Shaver being acquitted.

Eddie was never officially a part of the team, but he has a place with us. Since I can't be in court, he's agreed to wear a transmitter so Mia can follow along and give him guidance.

The stage is set.

My stage, that is. To bring Shaver down.

As we know, Shaver likes to stage his scenes, and this hit me harder than anything else. We haven't proven it yet, but if my theory is right about the staged crime scenes, then every one of Shaver's victims has a card.

I have a card. That makes me his victim. So where is my staged scene to take place?

My ultimate theory: Shaver is using the whole of DC as his staging ground.

I unroll a paper map across the glass conference table.

"Where did you even find this?" Mia asks. "I don't think I've ever seen a giant map in person."

Millennials. Which technically, I might be one—but I choose to believe you can grow out of it. Like there's a right of passage into generation X, and it's self-reliance.

"At a gift shop." I circle the downtown area. "We're going to focus our efforts here."

Charlie walks over. "Why do you think he'd keep Porter so close? That doesn't seem smart to me."

"Because Shaver needs to keep me in line. That means keeping her close enough that his someone on the outside can get me proof of life. He can't rely on technology, as his communications are being monitored, and he can't depend on his lawyer." Smigel hasn't proven to be a true troll. Not yet. "So he's relying on physical, tangible missives. That requires for whomever has taken Porter to be in close proximity."

The logic sounds reasonable. I'm not letting them know that, truthfully, I have no way to know this. It's conjecture. Two and a half days just isn't enough time to expand the search radius, and I need to focus my efforts *somewhere*.

"Charlie, pull up the card on the screen."

I had Mia enlarge and enhance it so we can see every

detail. For now, it's our only clue. More than that, it's our map.

I move closer to the screen.

Shaver's Tarot deck has to be old. I'm no historian, but my guess would be this card is at least half a century past its expiration. The details in the drawing are intricate. Hand painted. And that's where I'm getting lost, in the details.

"Is that a castle in the background?" I ask Mia.

"According to what I've researched, yeah. Every Five of Cups card across all decks presents a castle. Apparently, that's the cloaked man's destination, his prosperous future. If he can let go of his past."

I scrub a hand down my face. "Yeah. I know this. But where is that here?" I point to the map. "Shaver is pathological. With Tillman, his scene depicted her card—down to the eight stab wounds representing the eight swords. If the castle is the destination, that has to be where Porter is being kept. But there are no fucking castles in DC." I laugh dismally; I'm going to crack.

Mia looks uncertain. "How can you know that? Maybe you're being too literal. She could be anywhere. All Shaver has to do is label it a castle."

She's right. Dammit. "We're going in circles." Porter spoke the truth when she said I didn't evaluate Shaver long enough to get inside his head.

But he made damn sure he was inside mine.

He mentioned Melanie's accident. He asked about my history with Porter. He was either gathering intel, or gloating about what he already knew. How much information did he glean from Porter? They spent months prepping for his case. A sick hollowness twists my stomach.

"We need someone who knows him. Knows how he

thinks." I nod to Charlie at the computer. "Where's that asshole crony Lyle Fisher?"

"We weren't able to flip him," Mia says, worry creasing her kohl-rimmed eyes. "He could tell Shaver everything we're doing."

"And?" I turn to face her. "You don't think Shaver knows what I'm doing right now?" I check the time on my phone. We've already wasted the afternoon. "I have two days left before I have to testify. Fisher is the only person who knows this bastard, who might know where… Dammit."

"What?" Mia follows me to Charlie's station.

"It has to be him," I say. "Shaver could've planted Fisher with us to get information. Fisher has to be the one who was in Porter's apartment." *He took her*.

Charlie spins his chair around. "Dr. West, you can ask him yourself. Lyle Fisher is here. In the lobby. I had another interview scheduled for him today."

My head starts this annoying throb. I press at my temples. "Get him up here." Then I take hold of Charlie's chair, making sure he sees the seriousness in my eyes. "How illegal is it to interrogate someone?"

His dark eyebrows pull together. "Like torture?"

"If I have to go that far…"

Charlie looks unsure, as if he's suddenly seeing his boss for the first time. "If he knows something, we'll get him to talk."

"All right," I say, barely masking the disbelief in my voice. Charlie is my do-gooder. My black-and-white thinker. I've never witnessed him skirt the line before, and I have to admit, I'm a little rattled.

As we wait for Fisher, I pace the concrete floor.

The sheer helplessness of the situation feels as if the ground is crumbling beneath me.

"His castle," I say, thinking out loud. I look up at the screen. I need a focal point. If that damn castle is my figurative destination, I need to make it my literal one, too. "Okay. Let's pull up Shaver's financials. I want to know about every piece of property he owns."

I'll search every damn place in DC if I have to.

When Fisher enters the office, something snaps in my brain. I know that, medically, this isn't possible—but the *pop* happens just the same. My vision darkens, the crash of a wave detonates in my ears. The roar intensifies until all other sounds are too distant to hear as I thunder toward him.

I'm across the office and have the man by his throat. "Where is she? Where are you hiding her?"

There is no fear in his dark eyes. He makes a move toward his pocket, and I seize his arm. "I'm supposed to bring you a message," Fisher says evenly.

Charlie takes up my side and instructs Fisher to remove his hand slowly. He presents a phone and holds it up for me to take. Heart racing, I release Fisher and accept the phone.

"Hit the Play button," he instructs.

I stare at the device for a solid beat before glancing between Charlie and Mia. They are both motionless sculptures, waiting for me to press the button. "Don't let him leave. Tie him up if you have to."

Then I suck in a breath and start the video.

Porter's face appears on the shaky screen. My stomach bottoms out. Her hair is wild, mascara smeared beneath her eyes. The footage pans down, as if someone is adjusting the angle, and I glimpse blood-stained bandages wrapping her arms.

Where she was bled.

"West, I'm sorry," she says, her voice wavering. "I'm alive, but I don't know where. But I'm okay. Just do the right thing."

The frame drops. The video ends.

I clutch the phone so hard, the skin covering my knuckles burns. "Where the fuck is she?" I round on Fisher.

He shakes his head, dismissive. "You think he'd tell me? He gave me explicit instructions where to pick up the phone, and where to take it. That's all. I'm done." He holds up his hands. "That's all I had to do, and now I'm out. I'm not testifying. I won't."

I start toward him, and Charlie shifts in front of me. "Dr. West, think about this. Shaver wouldn't send you someone useful."

I don't want logic. I want to cause pain. I want this lowlife to bleed. I want him to tell me where Porter is.

"He goes nowhere," I say, as I circle the office table and refocus on the map. "Where did you get the phone? I want every bit of information your putrid brain can supply, and I want it now."

By one a.m., we've scoured Shaver's properties in the downtown area. I made three trips: an apartment complex, a bar, and a gym. All legitimate establishments, with residents and bookkeeping...but no sign of Porter. Fisher confirmed at least two of the businesses are being used to launder money for Shaver's drug dealings.

Which might help Eddie's case, but gets us no closer to finding Porter.

By morning, the question has to be asked. Is Eddie willing to throw the case if it's our only chance to save Porter's life?

I loathe that I'm the one to put this choice on Eddie, but Porter's running out of time. If Fisher does know anything, he's not talking. He won't turn on Shaver; he claims it's suicide, and he's probably right. But I'm officially out of shits to give for thugs. He might not have had anything to do with abducting Porter, but he works for Shaver. He's going to pay his dues one way or another.

I stand and stretch, then slide on my suit jacket.

"Where are you going?" Mia asks. She's been going over the footage from the trial today.

One screen displays the brief, panned shots of the jury that Eddie captured with the pinned cam to his tie, and the other screen shows stats on the jurors. Mia's own grading system for how likely a juror is to acquit versus sentence.

"I need to take a walk," I say. "Clear my head."

"It's late, Dr. West. You should get some sleep."

"Says the pot to the kettle."

"I never understood that."

"That's because you've never seen a kettle."

"Okay, well if you're up, take a look at this." She rewinds the trial footage and plays back Eddie's cross of Rendell. She's no longer the defense's star alibi witness; she's become a character witness for Shaver.

I know. The irony.

"It's only the first day, but majority of the jurors show favoritism to Eddie during his questioning."

Which would be a triumph for day one during any other case. "Who are the holdouts?"

"Well. The woman with a son—" she pivots to her jury

profile screen "—Sarah Jenkins. Her son is serving time in juvi for possession. Eddie's character assassination on Tillman didn't appear to go over well with her. Her expressions during the cross exposed her sympathy for Tillman."

I nod slowly. "Any way she's our jury foreman?"

Mia's eyebrows draw together. It's confusing, and difficult, to know which side to pull for. We can't let Shaver walk free, but his freedom is directly tied to Porter's life.

Mia shakes her head. "I doubt that. She works two part-time jobs. None of which demand much in the way of decision-making skills. I think she's under enough stress with family matters." She frowns. "But, I do have two that I'm leaning toward."

I brace my hands against the desk and lean closer to the screen. She pulls up two profiles, both I vaguely recall from *voir dire*. "Jackson and Smith."

Normally, I'd spend the night before trial studying the jurors' profiles. But I was with Porter. A blade to the heart.

"Camille Jackson is a tech firm CEO, and a likely candidate. And Andrew Smith, the high school history teacher, has experience in managing large, unruly groups."

I rub my eyes. "Like teens. That takes patience. An ideal jury foreman." The others would feel comfortable looking to him. His income isn't an intimidating insult, and teachers garner respect.

"The thing about Smith is," Mia says, as she slides to the second monitor, "he could sway either way. He seemed to be buying into Smigel's opening statement, but was slightly nodding along with Eddie's cross." She shakes her head. "Either I don't have a good read on him, or it's still too early."

I pat her shoulder. "It's still too early," I say in assurance.

Too early, but not for me. I'm running out of time. Porter's running out…too fast.

"I'm heading out. You get some sleep. I need your brain focused on tomorrow's sessions." I glance over at Fisher, not comfortable leaving Mia and Charlie alone with him. "I'll take him with me."

"Be safe," Mia says, then swivels back toward her monitors.

Once we hit the sidewalk, I turn toward Fisher. "Tell your boss that if he has Porter harmed in any way—" I close my eyes, visualizing the blood-soaked bandages covering her arms "—I'll end him. Maybe not now, or tomorrow. But I will end him."

Fisher tilts his head, searching. "You think he's afraid of death?"

His question jars me. All I can do is stare at the man.

Stuffing his hands in his pockets, Fisher braces for his walk. "Death is his favorite card, Dr. West. Good luck."

It might be the dumbest thing to let him walk away, but he's my only real link to Shaver and, therefore, Porter. He brought the phone, he brought the proof that—for now—she's alive. My instincts are skewed. My feelings for Porter distort my perception. So I have to trust in some other foreign thing that I used to mock.

Faith.

Maybe not intrinsic faith—but the trust that Shaver will use Fisher again to send a message.

I hurry my steps as I take the shortcut to Porter's apartment. I insert the key with a sinking feeling pulling at my gut. It seems like years since I was last here, not just this morning. Everything is still the way I left it. I'm not sure if I was hoping for change, for a new sign.

I turn on the lights and illuminate my phone flashlight. During my panicked search this morning, I might have missed something small, something important. Just one piece of evidence that could clue me in to whoever took her and where.

Damn. I should've brought Charlie. I need an investigator's eye. I flip up his contact, then toggle it away, thinking better of waking him. We need more than an eye; we need CSI-type shit. Finger dusting kits. Those special blue lights. Yeah, I'm not so good on the tech side of forensics. Not my department.

Tomorrow.

Porter will have been missing for twenty-four hours by the time the sun hits the sky. That's the official time I can report it. A thought hits me.

Porter's firm has to be questioning where she is. Right? Someone there can report her missing, and that's no violation on my part against Shaver. But who? I'm so out of the loop with her life that I don't even know who her friends are. What colleagues she's close with.

Porter has been benched. For at least another week. Will anyone notice her missing?

Someone *has* to be concerned.

I am. I'm the one who's missing her. I'm the one who Shaver knew he could manipulate. If for no other reason than his painstakingly meticulous nature, I know Shaver has saw to it that no one is worried about Porter. At least for the next couple of days.

I'm being torn in too many directions, and none of them have a definitive answer.

I enter the bedroom and shine the light around. The cups on the mantel catch the light. They're still positioned the same. Dread leaks into my soul.

Don't look.

But I'm compelled, like a magnet pulling me against my will. That's why I came here, right? Not to find some elusive piece of evidence. I came here to look in those cups and know that, when I take the stand, I have no other choice.

Step by step, I make it to the mantel. I use a tissue to remove the first goblet and peer inside. Empty, except for the remnants. A red wine-like stain lines the silver.

The first day is gone.

A tremor attacks my hand as I remove the second cup, my back teeth clenched. I embrace the anger instead of the pain. The coppery tang of blood hits me before I see the proof.

I nearly drop the cup. Leaning my head to the mantel, I pull in deep, steady breaths. My thoughts are not my own. I've become something...other. Desperate to inflict pain.

I'm going to kill him.

The bed is there, and that's where my body drops, giving up the fight.

SECOND CUP

DR. IAN WEST

Sunlight warms my face, and I squint against the overpowering brightness. For the second day in a row, I wake up in Porter's bed.

Buried in her down comforter, I inhale her lavender scent. There's a brief sense of rightness. Complete. Fulfilled. As I reach my arm out to draw her body to mine, I'm lost in that dreamy satisfaction, before reality crashes through the haze.

That internal alarm is triggered, and panic fuels my racked muscles to move. I scramble out of the covers, my bones made of cement. Every ache and pain comes alive as I pat myself down to locate my phone.

Head braced against my hand, I wait for Mia to answer. "Did you find anything on the phone that can help us?"

"Morning, Dr. West. Have you had coffee yet?"

I groan. "No. The phone, Mia?"

"It's clean. A burner. I'm sorry."

A defeated sigh escapes. I didn't expect Shaver to leave a

trail, but there's always a chance. He's delegating this thing from behind bars. Mistakes can be made.

This thought springs me out of bed completely, and as I end the call with Mia, I look at the cups. Even in my wrecked state, I used a tissue to touch them. Because of the chance for evidence.

I call Charlie and tell him to bring all his evidence collecting tools to Porter's apartment, then I check the time. Court starts in less than an hour.

I pace the hallway. Eddie picks up on the second ring. "What's going on?" he says. "Wait. I don't know if I can know this. Dammit. Just tell me something good."

"Make the deal." I let myself lean against the wall.

"What?"

"Set it up with Shaver. However you can. After I give my testimony tomorrow, I want Porter released right then."

Shaver made it clear that Porter would be kept until after the trial. *If* he was acquitted. I just need more time… I need Shaver to believe I've given up. But in the event I fail, I need Eddie on board.

The silence between us stretches, marking the actual distance. If it comes down to Eddie throwing the case, I'll lose Eddie's loyalty. He'll do it. Because he's one of the good guys, because he will have to do what's necessary to try to save Porter. But once it's done…we will be, too.

"All right, boss," he finally says. "I'll do my best. And, Ian. You don't have to feel guilty. After yesterday's sessions, this trial is looking pretty grim on my front."

I hang up, feeling guilty regardless.

Shaver has manipulated the system, and he may cost me a good friend. Eddie and I, our partnership, our friendship, will never be the same.

Impatient, I search Porter's cabinets for coffee while I wait for Charlie. By the time he arrives, I've ingested too much caffeine. But I'm awake. Alert.

Sleep on it.

It's what therapists say, and really, it's good advice for a reason. Our subconscious reveals problem-solving solutions while we give our conscious mind time off. I may not have the answer, but I have a destination.

I shrug on my suit jacket, decided.

Charlie pauses while putting on Latex gloves. "Where are you going?"

"To prepare my expert testimony."

For three years, I've come to this place on the anniversary only. But it's not where I talk to Mel. I said once that I don't have to…that she just knows…but that's not entirely true.

The actual truth is, I don't have to talk to a slab of marble, because I never *stop* talking to her.

She's always in my thoughts. I whisper offhand remarks to her as if she's still in the room. I mentally tell her about my day when I'm thinking about a case. I tell her I miss her all the time—because, God, I do. That constant ache that will never fully disappear is her unremitting presence in my life.

But I'm here now, because I need her in a way that only speaking openly, out loud and at her place, can grant me.

I kneel before her headstone and touch the cold marble. The witch charm I brought her is still here, and I reach inside my suit jacket and take out my flask. I set that next to the charm. The ache is fire in my chest. "You'd be so disappointed in me." I suck in a fast breath to staunch the burn in my eyes. "Porter got mixed up in something bad. I wasn't there for her. Now she's gone. I don't know how to help her, or where to find her. And what's worse..." I trail off, hating myself.

Shit. "I love her, Mel. You probably already knew this. But I love her. I always did; she's my friend, she's ours... she's family. She's a raging pain-in-my-ass on the defense team lately—but that doesn't change the way I feel. I'm sorry. I broke some rule, I'm sure. Some arbitrary rule about who you're allowed to fall in love with, and I'm sorry if I'm in the wrong, but it doesn't feel that way." My thumb glides across her name. "If it was really wrong, I wouldn't have been able to be with her. That sickness would've consumed me. The guilt would've torn me apart. But I felt none of that with Porter. Because you love her too, and you would want both of us to move on. You were the unselfish one, and I'm positive you've been trying to get me to see how I felt about Porter with all my annoyance with her—" I laugh.

"I get that now. And I'm here, talking to you like some crazy man, because I need your help." I pull the Tarot card from my jacket and lay it at the base of her headstone. "This was here for a reason. That sadistic fuck thinks he used your place to get to me, but really, you were trying to tell me something. As always, I was too stubborn to listen, but I'm open now. Tell me where she is, Mel. What am I missing?"

There's no answer. I'm not a fool, and I'm not delusional. I don't expect Melanie to swoop down on a bed of clouds and point the way. I'm not really sure what I do expect...

A sign.

More time.

Forgiveness, maybe.

For the pain to finally *stop*.

But that's not the answer, either. We feel pain for a damn good reason. Pain lets us know there is something wrong. We have to learn to listen to the pain instead of block it out.

I swipe my hand along the stone, and the jagged edge slices my palm. "Damn." I pump my fist, blood trickling from my palm. I start to untuck my shirt, to tear a strip to bandage it, when I look down at the Five of Cups.

A drop of blood pools on the card, right on top of the image of a bridge in the background. I pick it up to inspect closer. Wipe the blood away.

When that moment of comprehension seizes you, it takes your breath away.

I am a fool. The Fool Tarot card should've been my card, not the blasted cups. I've been thinking about Shaver's victims, the scenes he sets. *His* stage.

But it's not his; it's mine. The scene is linked to me.

And Porter.

"Thank you, Mel. You're still the smart one."

I tuck the card in my pocket and stand, nearly shaking with my certainty. I fumble my phone out of my pocket and call Charlie.

"Can your dad organize a search party?"

"Absolutely. When and where?"

I look off into the distance, marching toward my destination, my future. Yada fucking yada. *Fuck you, Shaver.* I always get the girl.

"The Yards Park."

16

THE CASTLE

DR. IAN WEST

I don't care how Shaver came about this knowledge. Whether I gave something away during our meeting, or if he probed Porter for the intel. Maybe he had us followed the night we came here together.

I can dissect that later. Right now, I only care that I find her in time.

It's like some bad action movie as I race toward the pedestrian bridge. I've got dirt and blood stains on my suit. People step aside, frightened of the wild-eyed man, to get out of my way. I don't slow to apologize. The closer I get, the heavier my feet become.

Fire snakes up my calves and I stumble, righting myself as I grasp the chain railing. A vise tightens around my lungs. I breathe through the pressure.

I stop just long enough to look around. I know this is where I'm supposed to be—but which side of the bridge do I cross? Where is the destination? As I climb the bridge, dragging my useless legs, I keep searching until I reach the center. There are buildings on either side of the bridge. *Which one?*

"Where are you, Porter?"

To my left is a wine distillery. And on the right is a boat landing. People mill around the distillery, too busy to keep a hostage. I cross the bridge.

This is me, *you fucking sadistic prick*, crossing my bridge! I might even shout it out loud.

My phone vibrates with a call from Charlie. "We're hitting The Yards now," he says.

"Damn. That was fast," I stammer out, breathless from the jaunt to get here.

"My dad has a search group on some local social media outlet that he keeps updated. Retired, but not dead. That's what he says. We have a scent dog, and I got Porter's scent from her laundry. We'll split into two smaller groups and start scouting either side of Riverwalk Trail."

I nod, as if he can see me. I'm nearing the boat landing and staring up at the buildings along the river. "I'm heading to the shipping yard." I swallow hard. "We'll find her. She's here. Thank you, Charlie." I end the call before the weight of my fear bleeds through the line.

I'll find her.

I take out the card and study it for the hundredth time, looking for some match on the buildings to the castle. A fucking castle. Now's not the time for sarcastic skepticism. My doubt can't hold me back.

A loud *bang* ricochets through the yard. A hydraulic crane lifts and deposits shipping containers onto the landing. Another *bang*, and it hits me with a sick twist of my insides —the utter realization of Shaver's plan.

I break into a run.

There are many—too many—shipping containers. I strain to see them all. They stretch across the landing, all the way into a massive warehouse. Panic stabs my chest. I text Charlie, because my voice can't be trusted. I tell him to bring the dog…to bring every last person.

She's here.

I start with the first container. Bolted. I knock on the side, then wait to hear movement within. But no. He wouldn't have her out in the open. *Think.*

Somewhere private.

I push past dock workers as I maneuver to the warehouse. It's a giant, rusted storage unit with tall bays and open-frame levels inside to store cargo. Lots of cargo. Sweat leaks into my eyes. I wipe at my forehead, then yank my jacket off.

It's like trying to solve a fairytale riddle. Where is the princess being held? In the highest tower? I scan the warehouse and mutter a curse. Then I start the climb, one rung at a time.

I bang on every container on my way up, fearing that it's pointless. That Porter's been drugged, sedated. *Or worse.* Fearing that I'm too late. Over twenty-four hours. How long can a person survive inside a container?

Shaver was never letting her go. After the trial, win or lose, her body was going to be moved and discarded. Like a piece of cargo.

The small search party enters the unit, and I wave down to Charlie. He points toward the other side of the warehouse. "We got a scent."

Every bone in my body liquefies under the swell of that crashing wave.

I'm down in a matter of seconds and heading up the back

of the search party. The dog steers us toward the middle of the warehouse before it stops, sniffing in circles.

"He lost the scent," Charlie explains. He looks frantic. That look detectives get when they're so close…

I glance up. "Give me the dog."

It's a risky climb up a ladder with a German Shepard (not a lap dog) under one arm, but I manage it at a slow, crawling pace. I hiss a fervent curse every time I miss a rung. At each platform, the dog hunts for the scent. The dog wines as I try to lift him again. He doesn't trust me. "I don't trust me, either, buddy."

"Hey you! What are you doing up there?"

I wipe at my forehead. "Cardio," I shout down. "What does it look like?"

Even from up here, I can tell the foreman isn't impressed. "Get the hell down. Now."

"Sir, that's not happening. I have four levels to climb and search, and you have a woman being held hostage in one of your containers."

Charlie sidles up beside me, the rest of the five-man search party spreading out on either side of the platform. I'm grateful for their back-up, as the burly foreman looks meaty enough to tear my limbs right off.

He removes his cap and scrubs a hand through his hair. "What the hell did you just say?" He whistles over to his crew. "Bring that lift."

Well shit. "That would've been a smarter and more proficient tactic," I whisper to Charlie.

"You're a trial consultant. Don't beat yourself up."

"Noted."

Within minutes, the titan of forklifts has the foreman lifted to our level. Charlie briefly explains that, we can have this place crawling with cops, or we can do the search ourselves. The man seems to frown at the idea of cops. No one likes cops, even if they have nothing to hide. It's a psychological tool implemented early on in adolescence.

The big man nods. "We'll help."

We resume the search, time wasted, but we make it up with the help of the crew and their much cleverer, convenient access to the containers.

By the time we're on the fifth row and nearing the top level, I'm drowning in sweat and despair. I realize I missed a call from Eddie. Only I can't talk to him. Not yet. Shaver is better at reading people than Eddie is at concealing his emotions.

I need Eddie to stay on track with the trial until…

Hands planted against a container, I squeeze my eyes closed. Bang my head against the corrugated steel. Trying to beat the defeated thoughts from my brain. "Dammit. Porter, where are you."

The sound is so slight, if I weren't frozen in my state of utter defeat, I might not hear it. I open my eyes and strain to hear. Another light *tap*. Then another.

I back away from the container, shaken. "Here!"

As the group nears, the barking picks up. The foreman stands in front of the container with a pair of bolt cutters, unsure. "If there's really a woman in here… Maybe we should get the police."

I'm not nearly as colossal as this man, and he can probably drop me dead with one solid right hook, but I'll be damned if I don't pummel my way right through him to get to Porter.

I snatch the bolt cutters from his hand and elbow my way to the lock.

Pure adrenaline and the desire to save Porter produces a Herculean strength I'd never obtained before. I bear down on the tool, teeth gritted, until I feel the hard snap as the lock gives.

Tossing the tool aside, I yank the lock off. Charlie and the guy are there to help me raise the door.

My heart stops.

The inside of the container is pitch-black. A flashlight is switched on. The beam roams the interior and lands on a huddled woman in the far corner.

There's a flurry of movement as people rush to get to her.

"Stop—" The order releases in a low, deadly tone. All movement ceases.

I push through the throng, my heart in my throat. I'm desperate to scoop her into my arms and hold her close, get her out of this place—but I have to assess her first. Make sure she's not injured, or in pain.

That she's alive.

"Everyone back up," Charlie says. "He's a doctor."

Well, I'm close enough. I kneel next to Porter and finally take a breath when I see her chest rise. *Thank you, God.* I push her tangled hair aside to inspect her face. She's bruised under her eyes, dehydrated. She blinks a few times, trying to open her eyes, but she's not lucid. I can tell by the way her head keeps dropping.

"I'm here," I whisper to her. I check the bandages on her arms. The blood is dry. She has other scrapes and contusions along her arms and face…and I shove my rage down into the boiling lava pit so I can evaluate the rest of her.

"Charlie, call 9-1-1," I say. "Get an ambulance here."

He jumps on it. "Is she all right?"

I swallow down another burning grief ball. "She's

drugged and dehydrated, but I think she's okay." I wrap her in my arms and cradle her to my chest. "Porter?"

She blinks up at me, straining to latch on to my features through the haze distancing her. But she's sees me. She knows I'm here. She's the most beautiful sight. I breathe her in, place my lips to her forehead. When her hand reaches mine and she grips my fingers, a racked sigh relieves the pressure as it tears through my chest.

"It's all right," I tell her, over and over, just holding on.

While we wait for the ambulance to arrive, I punch out a text to Eddie. *I have her. Destroy the bastard.*

THE DEVIL

DR. IAN WEST

No rest for the wicked.

That's the saying, right? That all the wicked, evil-doers are too busy plotting and destroying beauty to get a good night's sleep. Which makes sense, seeing as in order to pull off an elaborate corruption of the justice system, Shaver had to be controlling many moving parts.

He's been a wicked, busy bee.

The hospital swarms with nurses and patients. The hallway's a bustle of blue scrubs and white gowns. I'm seated in the corridor outside Porter's room. Not technically a room in the ER, she's behind the curtain, where I'm not allowed.

A serious-looking nurse with tired eyes tried to move me. And though I normally have enough compassion to commiserate with hardworking, tired nurses, that's not happening today. This woman was either going to have to Taser me, or get me a pass.

She got me a pass. Though I think she was considering the Taser.

I fiddle with the nametag on my rumpled dress shirt, thinking about all those moving parts, as I await Porter's update.

Two policemen and a detective already interviewed me, with the promise to return once they investigate more thoroughly. That means Shaver will be alerted soon that his scheme failed.

During the trial recess, I spoke with Eddie, filling in the blanks.

"Who does the container belong to? Who put it there?" he asked. Very good questions. Ones that I hope Major Crimes can trace back to Shaver.

Not that we don't have enough on him as it is to put him away for the rest of his twisted life, but again, it's those damn puzzle pieces. I'm not OCD by any means, but I like my cases solved. Absolutely. I like when all the parts align in a clear, concise picture.

What we do know so far: The shipping container was scheduled to be loaded onto a truck and moved this afternoon. I flash the home screen on my phone. 6:26 p.m. By this time, right now—had we been any later in getting to Porter—she would be gone.

The shock of that realization hasn't worn off yet.

I close my eyes. Breathe deeply, slowly.

According to the labs that have come back, Porter was dosed with propofol (or what the agitated nurse called a bolus), and an even larger dose of lorazepam, which is a generic sedative. A lethal cocktail that, if not administered correctly, could induce coma or death. But the perpetrator kept her alive, and under sedation for hours at a time. He kept her pliant and unable to fight.

That's a tall order of specific knowledge for a drug lord's crony.

Just one of the pieces that don't yet line up. Who would Shaver have under his thumb? A nurse? A pharmacist? A doctor? How could a person who clearly studied medicine, who's very first lesson is *do no harm*, sell their very soul in order to torture another human being?

Because, although Porter is recovering physically, make no mistake, the recovery time from the psychological aspect will take much longer. Porter was tortured.

Attacked in her home. Violently assaulted. Drugged.

Left alone for hours in the pitch-black, paralyzed, with only her fear.

I bury my head in my hands. Dig my fingers against my skull. "It's over."

I repeat this to myself. Over and over. I'm shaking, the lingering adrenaline still working its way from my system.

"It's over." Eddie's voice echos mine.

I look up. He's standing in front of me, hands in his suit pockets. The epitome of a satisfied prosecutor. He takes the seat beside me.

"How did you get a pass?"

He shrugs. "Working in the DA's office, you spend a lot of time in hospitals. The nurses like me here."

I nod knowingly, trying and failing to smile. It comes off more like an awkward grimace. *I'm trying*.

"You don't have to take the stand tomorrow," Eddie says, his tone reassuring. "Stay with Porter. I've spoken with Major Crimes. The shipping container was traced to one of Shaver's businesses. We have enough evidence to hang him."

I blow out a long breath. The trial feels a million light-years away. "What does Mia think?"

His mouth flattens into a hard line. Not a very convincing expression. "Mia thinks there's still a couple of jurors that are wavering. I don't get it, but she's the brains of the jury operation."

"The mother of the addict and the history teacher."

Eddie sighs. "That's the two. Maybe it's the adolescent angle. Both of them deal with kids, so there's some residual, protective thing going on there."

I crane an eyebrow, impressed. "Mia's rubbing off on you. Maybe you two should work together more often."

The slightest tinge of red flushes his face. "She's great. Really." His narrowed gaze slides my way. "But don't go there."

I bark a laugh, surprising myself. My neuroplasticity is showing again. The mind's ability to adapt in the face of adversity is amazing. Either that, or the wiring in my brain has short-circuited.

Stress can do that.

A solemn countenance washes over Eddie. "How is she doing?"

I watch as a nurse nearly tackles a man trying to leave the ER. I allow myself to get lost in the scene. "She'll recover," I say, distracted. I rub my eyes. "Thirty-one hours." That's how long Porter was inside that shipping container…waiting. Dying. So painstakingly slow.

He pats my shoulder. "She's strong. She'll be busting my ass in court again soon."

Work. That's what I need to focus on, at least until the warden of a nurse let's me see Porter. "What else can I do on the case."

It's not a question; it's a statement. More like a plea. Me begging Eddie to let me in—to give me a job. A role reversal for us that makes him speechless for a lapsed moment.

"Ian. You've done it all. Don't you get that? Shaver's never going to see the outside of prison because of you."

"It's still up to the jury."

He groans. "Let me worry about that this time. Mia has your back."

"How is the defense taking the introduction of all this new evidence?"

"Smigel is demanding a separate trial." He holds up a hand to stop any interruption. "But even if Judge O'Hare sides with the defense on this, we have him. Whether it's this trial or the next. He's going down."

There can't be a next trial. Because the next trial would involve Porter taking the stand as a witness. As a victim.

"Then you need me," I say. "I'm a credible, expert witness. Moreover, I have firsthand implications from Shaver. As I'm not on a legal team, my meetings with Shaver aren't bound by confidentiality."

But more than that, I need to look this sadistic bastard in the eyes and tell him he's lost.

"We'll see. Take tomorrow to spend with Porter. She needs a good doctor by her side." He smiles warmly. "There's plenty of time to testify if that's where we need to go."

I nod, unable, or unwilling, to debate the case. Eddie is a damn fine ADA. I want my moment, I want to take Shaver all the way down...but I also want to protect Porter. This time, from the very start.

Nurse Warden peeks her head through the curtain. "Dr. West, she's awake and asking for you."

Elation springs me out of the chair. Every tired bone forgotten.

As the nurse pushes aside a sheer panel, the beep of the heart monitor welcomes me inside the curtained cocoon. My heart gallops painfully inside my chest, racing, willing hers to beat stronger. Her slender body is wrapped in a nest of tubes and wires. She looks frail.

But her eyes… When her golden irises find me, every bit of tension cording my muscles dissolves. Shaver doesn't matter. The case, my company, all of it…gone.

This woman is my life. She's all I need.

I grab hold of her hand, stopping myself from gripping too tightly. The nurse points just outside the area. "Ten minutes, Dr. West. Then my patient needs rest."

I nod, my voice too choked.

Porter's thumb rubs my hand, that slight movement every ray of hope. I stroke her hair back from her forehead. The darkened skin beneath her eyes is starting to color again.

"I'm sorry," I hear myself say.

She tries to shake her head, but she's still weak. Her voice comes out even weaker, hoarse and cracked. "You saved me."

My eyes shut briefly. "Do you remember anything?"

Her throat pulses with a swallow. I reach for the cup on the tray, and she squeezes my hand. "I'm okay," she says. "No. Not really. Just glimpses as I faded in and out. When I woke up here, I wasn't sure if I'd been gone a day or a year."

Her words cut through me. There are no rehearsals for moments like this in life. Sure, movies supply us the tired, cliché phrases. And they work when we're at a loss; if we're too weary to try; if you're *that* guy. But I can't be, because Porter deserves better—she deserves honest.

"I was arrogant," I admit. I place my hand over hers,

encasing her slender fingers. They're so cold. "I took on Shaver during that first meeting like a conceited hotshot. I basically challenged him, dared him..."

She blinks up at me. "Do you really believe that? Because if you do, then you're even more arrogant than you think. Quentin Shaver was my client. He orchestrated all of this, and he didn't need your help or your challenge—" She breaks off, winded.

I prop the pillow behind her head, trying to be of some damn use. "You're right. Still, I should've known. With his pathology, I knew he was dangerous. I should've—"

"What? Insisted I remove myself from the case?" She frowns knowingly.

I match her derisive glare. *Touché*.

She coughs and attempts to sit up, but I lay a hand on her shoulder. With a sigh, she says, "It wasn't about you. I was his lawyer and it wasn't even about me. It was about *him*. He did all this for himself. And we can volley blame and guilt back and forth until we're *both* blue in the face, or we can move the hell on." She laces her fingers through mine. "You did save me, West."

I kiss her forehead.

"Inside that hell, all I could do was try to move and," she says, searching for words, "and talk to Mel. When I was lucid enough. Maybe it was the drugs, but I swear she heard me. And I swear...she told me you were going to save me."

A tear slips from the corner of her eye. I wipe her cheek. "I believe you." I do believe her, because without Mel, I would've found Porter too late, or not at all.

There is science, and then there is faith.

The two do not exist on the same plane. Just a week ago, had you tried to feed me some lame line about trusting in a higher power, I wouldn't have taken your case. I'm all about the science, the proof.

I can feel Mel rolling her eyes behind my back even as I think this.

I don't know what happened today, but I don't have to. And I don't have to prove it. Porter and I believe we're here because of a love we share for Mel. That's enough. That's a connection that will never be broken, no matter what happens between us.

She leans her face into my hand, seeking comfort. But then, just as suddenly, her face pales. "I have a card," she whispers.

Heart thumping erratically, I get closer. "What do you mean?"

"Oh, God. I didn't know if I was dreaming, dead, or what…but when I was able to keep my eyes open, I remember now. He wore a mask, and he had a card." Her eyes clench shut. Her words are rushed. "Some kind of devil mask. And the card was… The Lovers."

She's shaking. Tears well against her eyelids. Seeing her struggle to recall this horrid memory tears through me. "Hey. It's okay. It will come back in time." *I pray not.*

She shakes her head repeatedly against the pillow. "I'm not a snake," she says. "I'm not a snake…"

I clasp her face, forcing her to stop, and look into her eyes. "Whatever he said, it's not true."

Her lips tremble. "I don't remember it all. But I loved Mel, and I'm not a snake."

My breath releases hot through the fiery ache. Shaver will not have the last round—he will not torture her any longer. "You're caring and giving, and selfless. And you're the woman I love."

Her eyes close as she nods. She grips my hands. "I love you so much, West. Tell me it's over."

"It's over, Porter." I caress her cheek. "You don't have to think about it, and you don't have to fight to remember. He's a liar, and he's the snake. Let your brain rest. The mind blocks painful memories when we're too weak so we can focus on healing. You never have to recall anything. Just heal."

A quivering smile tugs at her mouth. "You're shrinking me."

"I am. But it's the truth. Don't think about it ever again." I place a tender kiss to her lips.

She sighs in relief as she relaxes. "I've never seen you so serious. Stop it."

I laugh. "You want the arrogant dick back? Will that make you feel better?"

"Yes. At least I know what to do with that guy." She attempts a wink. If it wasn't for the pain she's suffering, it would be adorably awkward.

"I have plenty for you to do to me later." I kiss her again.

As she drifts off, I stand watch over her. Porter is strong. Resilient. She'll balance between good days and bad as she heals—physically and mentally—but her ability to relate and joke marks a positive starting point.

Still, something bothers me. I move toward the containers holding her clothes. I do a quick search, looking for the Tarot card. It might be a suggestive memory, her mind mixing the facts of the case and her abduction. Or it could have even been a drug-induced hallucination. Or a psychosomatic result of anxiety.

Her pockets are empty. Nothing in the bins.

Adrenaline officially vacated, I nearly collapse. I catch

the wall and ease myself down along the floor. The nurse comes in to check and, she must think I'm the most miserable soul to ever grace her ER, because she simply frowns and leaves me a rumpled mess on the floor.

Shaver gave me a card because, as he put it, I had a purpose. I was a player in his twisted scheme. He may be deluded enough to believe the cards give him a more profound purpose other than his compulsion to kill, but the fact is, Porter was merely a chess piece to him, his pawn, to move me around the board.

She doesn't fit his victim profile. If Shaver gave her a Tarot card, it'd be on her person. Shaver needs that psychological control over his victims.

He wore a devil mask.

Death is his favorite card.

All summed up by Shaver's infatuation with the Arcana. That's all.

I rest the back of my head against the wall, listening to Porter's even breaths. When my choice is clear, I steel my resolve and find Eddie.

18

FULL CIRCLE

DR. IAN WEST

I hold up my right hand, left placed on the Bible, as the registrar swears me in.

My gaze is fixed on Shaver at the defendant's table, my words directed toward him. His dark eyes alight with a grin that doesn't match the rest of his severe expression, but I can feel his amusement. Because that's what this is to him; a game. Another move on the board.

Only it's not a move on my part. It's checkmate.

I stand in the witness box and recite my credentials. Then Eddie approaches. We rehearsed this briefly just a couple of hours ago. But—pardon my pun—I have a literal card up my sleeve that he's not aware of.

"Good morning, Dr. West. During your evaluation of the defendant, were you able to determine whether or not Quentin Shaver is of rational and sound mind?"

I look to the jury to answer. "I was. And he is."

Eddie nods. "You were able to do this with only an hour-long assessment?"

"Yes. Along with my evaluation, I ordered an MRI and CAT scan to determine if there was any significant brain trauma that would warrant further study into Mr. Shaver's behavior." I lock eyes with juror number seven. Our history teacher and assumed jury foreman. "Mr. Shaver passed with flying colors. He has never suffered any brain damage. Therefore, my conclusion is that Mr. Shaver was completely aware and in control of his actions when he murdered Devin Tillman. To which he planned and executed, in my professional opinion, meticulously."

"Thank you, Dr. West. What is your official diagnosis of the defendant?"

"Quentin Shaver displays clear signs of psychopathic tendencies and antisocial personality disorder. In short, he feels no remorse or empathy for his victims. Shaver stalked Ms. Tillman, then manipulated her. When his compulsion to make her a part of his Tarot fantasy couldn't be contained any longer, he bound her, tortured her, and murdered her. Then he staged the murder scene to resemble the Eight of Swords Tarot Card."

Eddie clicks the remote in his hand, and an image that Mia spliced together appears on the large monitor. One side is a portrait of the Eight of Swords Tarot card, the other side is a picture of the Tillman crime scene.

A burst of shocked disbelief rolls through the courtroom. I filter out the murmurs and gasps. I'm not here to impress the court; I'm intent on watching the jury, logging every reactive expression as they stare at the screen.

They see it. They can't deny the evidence; it's right in front of their faces. It just needs a name.

"This is Shaver's MO," I say, speaking over the subtle commotion. "A combination of Shaver's method and motive."

There it is, folks. Motive.

The proverbial nail in the coffin.

Smigel is right on cue as he bounds out of his seat. "Your Honor, objection. Extreme prejudicial speculation. Dr. West is not a member of law enforcement, and therefore doesn't have the credentials or skills to make this assessment."

Eddie speaks up. "Dr. West has worked in the field of forensic psychology, Your Honor."

"Overruled," Judge O'Hare says. "As Dr. West does in fact work closely with officials and has previous experience, I would like to hear more of this theory." Bushy white eyebrows raised, Judge O'Hare motions for me to continue.

"It is pure speculation," I admit, then look right into juror number three's eyes. The mother of the addict. "However, when something is just too damn obvious to ignore, how can we?" She frowns, but she knows. Guilt is a powerful tool.

Smigel barely gets his objection in before the judge slams the gavel. "The jury is instructed to disregard Dr. West's statement." His gaze zeros in on me. "I'm being lenient with you, Dr. West, but if you try my patience, I'll have you removed from my courtroom again. Understood?"

Ah. So the man does have an excellent memory. "Yes, sir, Judge O'Hare."

"Good. Mr. Wagner, please proceed." He points a deliberate finger at him. "And I warn, cautiously."

"Yes, Your Honor. Thank you." Eddie rubs his chin. His signal that he's about to go for the jugular. I can take it. "Dr. West, do you, in fact, have any law enforcement credentials or training?"

"No. Not at all."

He nods. "So your evaluation of Mr. Shaver is purely based on the hour you spent with him, correct?"

I sit forward, so every member of the jury can see me clearly. "No. Officially, I had three meetings with Mr. Shaver. My observation went further when he had my girlfriend, Mr. Shaver's former attorney, Porter Lovell, abducted and tortured for thirty-one hours in a shipping container in order to manipulate me into giving a false testimony."

"Objection, Your Honor!" Smigel springs to his feet. He waves his hand around, seeking the right words. "Objection to…all of it. This is ludicrous. Hearsay. Facts not in evidence. Speculation—"

Judge O'Hare motions for the defense lawyer to stop. "I get it, Mr. Smigel. I want all counsels to approach my bench *now*."

I swivel to face the judge as Eddie and Smigel advance.

Smigel starts. "This is a deliberate attempt by the DA's office to poison the jury, Your Honor. Dr. West's theories are a part of a current, ongoing investigation, and there is a motion in place that forbade mention of any part of the investigation or Ms. Lovell's situation during this trial."

Judge O'Hare frowns as he directs his attention to Eddie. "Is this true, Mr. Wagner?"

"It is, Your Honor, and the DA's office is complying with the motion. However, Dr. West is not citing hearsay from the investigation. This is his direct, firsthand experience with the defendant, and should be admissible."

The judge attempts to mask his disgust as he turns toward me. "Is Ms. Lovell all right?"

This cinches my heart. No matter the rules, she's one of

them—one of us. She's a reminder to the judge that, sometimes, the system fails us. "She is recovering, Your Honor. And, if I may, I am giving my firsthand testimony so that Ms. Lovell can be spared taking the stand in her condition."

Smigel scoffs. "Your Honor, see? This can't be allowed. This evidence clearly belongs in a separate case—"

"That's enough, counselor." The Judge considers his options for a moment. "All right. I'll allow Dr. West to speak to his experience in relation to the defendant only." He inclines his head my way. "Don't cross that line, Dr. West, or I will hold you in contempt."

"Duly noted, Your Honor."

Smigel is not pleased as he resumes his place behind the defense table. I straighten my tie, wondering how much this is going to cost me in fines. We might need a *Get Ian out of Jail* fundraiser.

Eddie moves before the witness stand and braces his hands on the edge. "Dr. West, during your assessment of Mr. Shaver, did he make any threats directed toward you or Ms. Lovell?"

"Yes," I answer. "Specifically, after I discovered Ms. Lovell missing from her apartment, during my second meeting with Mr. Shaver—and I paraphrase—he asked me how I saw my cup—" I glance at Shaver, then to the jury "—whether I viewed it as half full or empty, as my answer would determine whether Ms. Lovell lived or died."

The appall on the jurors' faces is enough. That's the expression I want; that's the emotion that will make sure Shaver doesn't walk away a free man.

Eddie nods to me. "Thank you, Dr. West. No further questions."

Judge O'Hare can't help but shake his head as he instructs Smigel on his cross examination.

I square my shoulders, braced, as the lawyer lines me up in his sights and moves in. Oh, the troll wants to take me down. This should be fun.

"Dr. West, isn't it true that psychologists are required to keep their sessions with patients confidential?" Smigel asks.

So, he's going for the ethical card to try to discredit me. "This is true," I say, "except for in the case of court mandated evaluations and threats of harm made against the psychologist."

Smigel scowls, brow creased in hard thought. "During your recent meeting with Mr. Shaver, did you attack him?"

There's an expectant pause, where the judge and the whole courtroom prepare for an objection from the prosecutor. It never comes, however. This is good reality TV drama right here. Who wants to interrupt this?

I speak into the mic. "I did. Absolutely." I lift my hand and make a fist. "I stuck this fist right in his face when he refused to give me the location of where Porter Lovell was being held against her will."

Ethical? No. But the jury doesn't care about ethics. They're people. They're human. They *commiserate* and identify with me. What if it was their loved one? What would they do? Eleven out of twelve would want to do exactly what I did, or worse.

And this isn't about me, Eddie, Smigel, or the judge. It's all about the jury.

Smigel knows this and, as he glances at the jury, decides to change tactics. "Dr. West, you maintained that the defendant acted on some compulsion pertaining to his pathology."

I raise my eyebrows. "Yes, that's correct."

His nod is slow, leading. "In theory, if this speculation is true, wouldn't Ms. Lovell be a part of this proposed Tarot fantasy?"

I see where he's going, and he wants me to stumble. "In theory, but she wasn't. Let me explain—"

"I see. So, in theory, according to you, we have a pathological and meticulous killer who keeps to a particular method, and you're saying he broke his own MO?" He looks at the jury, resonating doubt. "In your experience, how often do ritualistic offenders deviate from their MO?"

Son of a bitch. "Rarely, but in this case—"

"Thank you. Now, Ms. Lovell is a fine defense attorney. However, to your knowledge, has she won every case she's presented?"

"I don't believe so"

"So, it's possible Ms. Lovell has disgruntled clients, then. Some who may have been convicted of crimes with expensive fines or served a prison sentence due to her failings?"

"It's possible."

He's going for the illusory suspect. Typically, a defense attorney will try to point the finger at another possible suspect to cast reasonable doubt on the defendant. If it's possible that someone else orchestrated the crime, then it's possible the defendant is innocent. Therefore, doubt.

"And, to your knowledge, where was Mr. Shaver during Ms. Lovell's abduction?"

"In court holdings."

He nods, pleased with himself. I peek at the jury to get a quick eval. They don't like his smug attitude. Still, they're open to consider the facts. This is a smart jury.

Smigel doesn't let up. "You stated before that you're in a romantic relationship with Ms. Lovell. Is that correct?"

"Yes."

Smigel paces before the witness stand, getting his lawyerly groove on. "In your experience, do romantic feelings cause conflicts of interest in the work place? Say, where your feelings for Ms. Lovell may skew your evaluation of the defendant, or inflame you to point the finger at the defendant without any solid evidence?"

Eddie snaps to attention. "Objection. Compound and leading, Your Honor."

"Sustained. Let the witness answer a question, Mr. Smigel."

"Sorry, Your Honor." He swipes a hand through the air, urging me to answer. "Can romantic feelings cloud judgment, Dr. West?"

"Of course," I say. "Let me go ahead and answer the rest for you, as well. When it comes to Porter Lovell, I am a mess of a man. I admit that. I've apparently been in love with her for the past three years, and too stubborn to see it."

A woman on the jury inhales deeply. Everyone can sympathize with me being a dumbass in love.

"But that doesn't change the facts of what I've witnessed and know," I add. "Quentin Shaver requested a meeting with me during his previous trial where he alleged vague threats if I didn't declare him temporarily insane as an expert witness. He then made good on those threats when Porter was taken. He confirmed this was his doing by proxy when I confronted him."

Smigel observes me closely. "According to you, that is. A psychologist who, for the woman he loves, takes the stand and breaks an ethics oath to reveal a patient's session."

Oh, Smigel. We already covered this. He thinks by reiterating his viewpoint, repeating lies, the jury—who is vastly becoming bored—will be swayed.

Time for a magic trick to wake them up.

"Actually, according to Shaver himself." I reach into my jacket inseam and reveal the bagged Tarot card. *Tada*. I hold it up and flip it around, displaying the note Shaver slipped into my pocket during our altercation. I explain this briefly.

Smigel practically vaults to the stand to try to snatch the evidence bag. But I'm faster, moving it to the judge's bench. "Your Honor, I'm sure the ADA would like this admitted into evidence. I received this missive from the defendant after my third meeting with him."

Smigel makes his argument, but Judge O'Hare, after looking over the card and note, admits them both into evidence, with the stipulation they are to be evaluated by both opposing counsels.

Then the judge takes over the questioning. "What is this card, Dr. West?"

"The Five of Cups Tarot card, Your Honor." I tell Judge O'Hare and the jury about where it was discovered, and Shaver's confession of having the card delivered to me by proxy. "Before Mr. Smigel moved the questioning on too quickly, I was going to state that no, Shaver's victim was not Ms. Lovell. In fact, I was his intended victim."

I meet Shaver's gaze across the courtroom. His mouth kicks up into a crooked smile. His arrogance hasn't wavered. *That's mine*, he mouths. I can only assume he refers to the card. He claims he always returns the cards to his deck.

Not this time, I answer back.

Regardless of where I sit, having beaten him by his own rules, Shaver is still trying to intimidate me. As if the fortune this card holds has some kind of power over me. But I faced it, didn't I? I followed the path, I crossed the damn bridge, I climbed the fucking tower. *I win, asshole.*

The judge places the card and missive into evidence, then instructs Smigel to wrap up his questioning.

"I have nothing further, Your Honor."

With that, Judge O'Hare calls a recess, and I step down from the witness stand.

As I pass the line of jurors, I take a brief assessment. Despite my damning testimony, there is still one possible holdout from our foreman Smith. But I know it's because he's waiting for the science. He's a teacher. Facts are important.

Right before the jury is dismissed, the history teacher catches my eye, giving me a slight nod. Validating my performance.

Does this change his mind? Not for the first time today, I wish I had Mia in my ear. I need her insight. Mouth pressed in hard assertion, I try to find the thread that altered his opinion so quickly. Even now, he's difficult to read.

Either way, once the science prevails, we'll have the support of the entire twelve jurors.

It started here. It ends here.

Game over.

19

TWO WEEKS LATER

DR. IAN WEST

Recap time.

Let's make this brief, because I have plans.

Okay—let's see. The trial concluded this week. The verdict was handed over by the jury on Wednesday, citing a unanimous guilty judgment to the first degree murder of Devin Tillman.

After expert handwriting analysis, and days of counter expert testimony trying to debunk the analysis, in the end, Shaver provided—literally, in his own hand—the damning evidence that convicted him.

It was the *her blood will spill* line that cinched it.

Once Shaver's method was established, the link between the Tarot card and crime scene paved the way for Eddie to enter the motel DNA as evidence. There was very little doubt Smigel could create after that. Shaver was in that room. His DNA was found on Devin Tillman's body.

Nail. In. Coffin.

Upon his conviction, the media dubbed Shaver the Arcana Killer. Catchy, right? Typically, a killer has to be found guilty of at least three murders before he gets a moniker, but once the details of the trial reached the press, the connection between Shaver and his Tarot card staged crime scenes went viral.

There are other scenes, other victims. Major Crimes has connected at least two other murder victims to Shaver's MO, and they're heavily investigating to gather evidence to prove it.

Lyle Fisher did testify. He admitted to delivering the Tarot card to Melanie's gravesite, but not to any knowledge of Porter's abduction beforehand. He was a pawn. As such, he was granted immunity for his testimony.

But that doesn't mean we've stopped investigating him.

Judge O'Hare sentenced Shaver to life without parole. He presented a lovely closing speech that gave me chills, describing Shaver as the most gruesome monster to ever desecrate his courtroom.

It was quite fitting, seeing as Halloween is just around the corner.

Tonight is the eve of, in fact.

After forensics tested the evidence, I had to decide what to do with my property. The card and the cups at Porter's apartment proved useless after they were processed. No prints, no DNA. So I took the card, and told them to melt the damn cups.

I don't know why I kept it. Other than some morbid proof; a reminder not to go down the wrong path again. Or some shit. I don't know. Shaver wanted the card, so I kept it from him. Simple as that.

During his transfer to a maximum security prison, Shaver

was attacked by another transfer inmate and stabbed three times with a makeshift knife. Two superficial flesh wounds, and one fatal puncture wound to the liver.

Shaver was transported to a hospital where he died during surgery.

He didn't serve one day of his sentence.

Justice or injustice?

Only his victims can answer that for sure.

Kind of an anticlimactic ending, I know. But the one assurance this brings is that Shaver no longer poses a threat to Porter, or anyone else. He can't manipulate anyone from behind bars like a psycho puppet master. That fear is alleviated. Gone.

Porter was released the afternoon I took the stand against Shaver. With her physical condition improved, and tests confirming she was out of danger, she demanded her release, making arguments against being kept against her will.

The hospital staff was more than delighted to give her a clean bill of health and send her on her chipper way.

Porter gave the firm her notice, giving up the partnership, and came to work with the good guys. She officially started today, bringing a case with her that she picked up while in the ER. I told you before, the woman is relentless.

Even though the trial is over, and Shaver is dead, the team is still working the Arcana angle to help recover more victims. It's the victims that matter; giving closure to the families.

Oh, you were hoping for something more exciting, like a twist? Yeah, honestly, me too. I'm still moving around the parts in my head as the team and Major Crimes tries to narrow down the proxy perpetrator who abducted Porter. Fisher is the most likely suspect, but he actually has an alibi that checks out. There are many Shaver associates to investigate, so I have faith we'll find the person. We're getting closer.

I know that, even though she won't admit it aloud, Porter will feel safer once she has this permanent closure. There are moments when I catch her staring off, listless, before a shudder takes her. Like she just recalled a memory, or she's trapped in that container again, her mind held prisoner.

I do my best—as a psychologist, as the man who loves her—to bring her out of these trances safely, and to help her keep moving forward.

That's what my plans are about. Now that we're free of the trial, and Shaver is buried six feet below, I'm taking Porter away from DC. A short trip to a B&B where, for two days, we leave lawyering and trial science and criminals behind. Two days that belong all to us.

I gather my briefcase and phone from my desk, then look around the office. It's a peculiar feeling to leave it vacated for even a weekend. I sent Mia and Charlie home earlier, demanding they take time off to recoup before we start the new case on Monday.

"You look so lost."

Porter leans against her desk, the one we placed next to Mia's. It's like it always belonged there. "I'm not lost. I'm just…thinking."

She walks toward me, those sexy hips swaying in that damn tease of a pencil skirt. Her arms link around my neck. "What are you going to do with two whole days off work?"

I slip my hands to her waist with a long, exaggerated sigh. "Oh, I'll be working." I kiss her wrist. "I'll be working here." I move to her neck. "And here…"

She laughs and slips away. "I am not starting that here,

with all these mics and cameras around. Mia's tech freaks me out. I'm going home. To sleep." She gives me a quick kiss before attempting to walk off.

I grasp her hand. "Wait. I'll walk you home."

She crosses her arms, defenses on high. "I'm fine, West. You don't have to keep being the hero. I can walk myself home." And she's off again.

I snag her arm and bring her to me, where I clasp those hips I adore and plant her right on my desk. "Listen here," I say, taking her face in my hands. I tilt her head back, look into her golden eyes. "I know you can handle yourself and that you don't need me to save you or protect you."

She licks her lips. "All right, then. Settled. Let me down."

She tries to wriggle free, but I move in closer. Hold her tighter. "But I want to," I say, stroking her jaw tenderly. "You saved me first, Porter, and I will want to save you every day from here on out. I need to, so give that to me. I want to be your hero the way you're already mine. Please tell me you'll have me."

Her eyes shimmer, and as she struggles to blink away the wetness, her breaths come uneven. "Stop making me love you so damn much. I don't know if my heart can take it."

I smile. "I know the feeling." I kiss her deeply, the ache in my chest overwhelming, crushing. I will never take this for granted. I will never miss a day where I tell her how much she means to me.

Loss and grief breaks you—but it also forges a new path through the pain, if you let it—one where you appreciate every new chance to love again.

Yes, I know. I've turned into a sap. I might even be a little whipped. But damn it feels right. Just like my hand on Porter's thigh as I ease upward.

"Is that sexy lace thigh-highs I feel?"

Her smile—that sly minx smile I love—curves her lips.

I groan. "That's it. Let's get you home. Now." I'm might be a sappy man, but I'm still a man. I walk Porter to her apartment, gloating that I actually won an argument with her, until she shuts me up.

20

FATE

I flip on the light and toss my keys on the table as I trek to my kitchen. Before I start to pack, I pour two fingers of bourbon into a tumbler. I'll need this.

The cup just reaches my lips when an eerie feeling trails the back of my neck, making the hairs lift away from my skin. That's not a feeling to ignore. Thousands of years of survival instincts delivered in one punch.

I see it then—the silver cup on my bar counter.

"I was hoping you'd choose my cup. But I guess cravings are stronger than reason."

I whirl around, the bourbon splashing my hand. A man is sitting in my mother fucking living room. "Who the fuck are you, and why are you in my apartment?"

He stands, then gradually moves into the slant of light. I recognize him. Andrew Smith. The history teacher.

"You're not supposed to be here," I accuse. "You're a member of the jury."

"The case is over," he says nonchalantly.

I take a hard swallow of alcohol before I set the glass

down. "You have exactly five seconds to tell me what the hell you're doing here before I call the cops." I take out my phone and hold it up.

"You have something of mine. It's time to return it."

I squint at him, then glance at the silver cup. The floor beneath my feet shifts. The air vacates the room, my lungs deprived of oxygen for the briefest moment as realization collides.

All those moving parts... They slam together in one epic grand finale.

I move to my left, putting the table between us. Giving myself a second to think.

The motel DNA. Since the start of the case, I wondered how Shaver made such a careless mistake. A beginner mistake. Toss around enough synonyms, and we get rookie... novice...apprentice.

Smith is a history teacher...

The answer dings inside my skull like a bell.

Teacher and pupil.

"So which one are you?" I ask. "The master or apprentice?"

His smile tips one side of his mouth up, as if my question is only slightly amusing to him. "You've done your research, but I wouldn't expect anything less of the great Dr. West."

"All right, then. Master, I presume. Just tell me how the hell you wormed your way onto my jury?"

"Your jury?" He chuckles. "The biggest delusion we believe is that we have any control whatsoever."

Me. I'm the one who put him on the jury. I failed to see what was right in front of me. He manipulated *voir dire*, but I'm the one who was supposed to see through the act. I didn't, and he slipped right past us, all because I wanted a foreman who I could easily read.

He set me up.

And I let him.

Which begs the question: "If Shaver's your apprentice, or student...lackey?" I give my head a mocking shake. What's his button? "Then why didn't you sway the jury to find Shaver innocent? I mean, that's why you were there. To make sure the trial went your way and not mine, right?"

A puppet master who needs to control everyone and everything. I should've seen through Shaver—I should've seen that he was lacking.

Smith is medium height. Short brown hair. Ordinary and unassuming. This man can get lost in a crowd. Overlooked. It's so blatantly obvious now—but isn't it always? When we're fed the answer later? When we're just too damn late?

In retrospect, I was preoccupied with Porter. Falling for her...saving her.

This man found my button on day one.

He fans a hand over the table, inviting *me* to sit at *my* table. Ballsy.

"I'll stand. Thanks."

He shrugs and pulls a chair out to sit. He folds his hands on the table, comfortable. Not worried about what I'll do in the least. "Shaver was supposed to be the answer. I get... tired. Having an apprentice to take over seemed like the solution."

"Did your cards tell you this?" I'm trying to analyze just how delusional this man is, and thereby how dangerous. The door is a few feet away, but I can't leave. We both know this. He has answers. But what's more, I can't leave behind another threat to Porter.

"Yes," he says. "The cards pointed me to Shaver. But it wasn't until his sloppy work got him caught that the real reason I chose him was revealed. The cards are never wrong. But at times, they can be mysterious. I have immense patience, however."

Play into his delusion. Keep him talking calmly. I'm trying to assess him and the situation…but my mind is overloaded. The one thing—the main thing—I want to do is wrap my hands around his neck and end the chance he'll ever get near the woman I love.

"It was you. You took Porter," I say as it comes to me. "You twisted fuck. You watched us together, then you waited —like a coward—for me to leave. Then you took her."

He *tsks*. "You're getting ahead of yourself, Dr. West. We'll get to that. I need you to understand something vital first."

My shoulders tense. "What…Smith? I also presume that's not your name?"

"To you it is. But that's not important. What you need to understand is that Shaver wasn't the answer. You were. The man in the cloak." A beat. "Shaver led me to you, so I forgave his tiresome blunders. Until he was no longer useful."

Shaver would be able to appeal and try to make a deal if there was proof another killer was involved with the murders. This man—*Smith*—made sure that couldn't happen.

Suddenly, the card I carry in my pocket feels like it might burn a hole through my skin.

Smith studies me, head tilted. "You have the card, I presume."

I say nothing.

His smile is knowing. "Of course you do. It's your trophy,

Dr. West. Killers keep them to recall their precious memories of their victims."

"I'm not a killer, you deluded bastard. And now, since this is going nowhere, I'm making that call."

"No, you're not. Because I have something even more valuable to you." He dips a hand into his pocket, and I tense…waiting…until I glimpse the white corner of an envelope. "The man you're looking for, the one who kidnapped Porter, is Gregory Miller."

Confusion pulls my eyebrows together. I don't like not having the answers beforehand. I try to work it out before I say anything, but Smith offers the answer first. He's running this show. For now.

"Gregory is a nurse at the downtown hospital. He might have even passed you in the hallway while running tests for Porter. Such a small world."

"Why are you snitching on your accomplice?"

His smile lights his dark eyes. "Gregory is in my safekeeping. You won't find him. Not without this…" He fans the envelope.

"What do you want from me? Other than your damn Tarot card."

His features darken. "I want my salvation, Dr. West."

Shaver said the same thing during his evaluation. "What does that mean?"

He only smiles. Then: "Gregory was an intern three years ago," he continues, as if we have all the time in the world. "Do you know how many hours interns sleep during a week? Approximately twenty. They stay up for hours, downing coffee to stay awake, while in that first year of training." He shakes his head. "That's ironic, isn't it? They train to save lives, and yet, their very duty-bound drive makes them a hazard to those they deem to save. Well, it makes them a hazard on the road, anyway."

My legs go weak. Shaking, I plant my hands on the table. *No. He's a liar.*

"You're an intelligent man, Dr. West. I'm sure you're linking the pieces together."

My knuckles ache as I try to steady myself, teeth gritted. "You're lying."

Features masked, he remains a still reed at the insult. "Am I? There was a witness to Melanie's hit and run. The police report redacts this information to protect the identity. Finding the witness was easy. All you need is a person who can provide the full report. Now, getting this witness to confess to what they *really* saw was a bit trickier. At the time, they didn't want to get involved, so lying came naturally. But pain doesn't. Pain breaks the most stubborn wills." His gaze narrows on me, scrutinizing. "Wouldn't you agree?"

He tortured the eye witness to find the driver's identity. I reach for appall—but there's a dark, shallow part of me that is envious, that despises myself for lacking the ability to have done this myself.

"Pain can make a person insane," I say. "I see it's worked wonders on you."

He shrugs. "You can try reverse psychology, but it won't give you what you want. I'm already offering you answers." He sits back, lifting his head higher. "What Shaver told you about the gypsy was true. It was my story he fed you, along with every tantalizing detail and clue. You were just too blinded by your own pain to see it then. But now you can."

I wedge another piece of the puzzle into place. "So you blackmailed this Gregory guy to lock Porter in a shipping container. To drug her and torture her…"

"It's true. We all cave when confronted with the demons of our past. Gregory was haunted by his, tortured by the fear that his sin would become known. Therefore, he was willing to take a second woman's life, rather than repent for the first."

Rage covers my vision.

Smith reveals a Tarot deck, shuffles it leisurely. Then flips over a card. "The Lovers."

Porter's card.

"You still have it." A mix of fear and relief edges my voice. "You didn't give her the card."

"Porter wasn't haunted by her demons. She was carrying yours. It seems together, you set each other free." He slips the card back into the deck. "Very inspiring."

She's safe. I hear nothing else.

"I'm not a monster, regardless of what you may think," he says. "If you dig deeper into my *victims*, you'll see what I see, what the cards see—all the pain and torment. Lives haunted by the unforgivable actions of their past. The cards give them a path, a choice, but it's up to them to accept their fate."

My head spins. I clutch the edge of the table, grounding myself. "And what do you believe is my fate?"

His gaze bores through me. "You've come so far…you're so close."

"Tell me!"

"It was never Porter's blood that was meant to spill, Dr. West. Your cup will always remain half empty, no matter how much you love Porter. No matter how much you strive to move on. You are a haunted man, because Melanie's killer was never brought to justice."

I shake my head.

"Yes. Your demons are screaming inside you now. That's

why you punish the wicked. Trying to silence their voices. But there's only one way to quiet them."

"No."

He holds up the envelope in a taunt. "Accept your fate, Dr. West, and become my apprentice. Become my salvation."

I laugh. The sound leaves my constricted throat in a strangled mock. "I'm not your puppet." I lift my chin, forcing bravado. "Your cards lied to you."

"Oh. They never lie." He makes to stand, and I raise the table and slam it down.

"Give me the envelope," I demand. I grip the edge of the table, envisioning ramming it into his throat.

He slips it between his fingers. "Of course. It's my gift to you. You're the only one to ever come this close, Dr. West. You looked into the monster's eyes and faced your fear, faced your bones."

I release a tense breath. "You're a delusional psychopath who will spend the rest of his life locked in a white, padded room. Now give me his fucking location."

He stands, but all I can see is that envelope in his hand. "What will you do with it?"

My gut clenches as too many prospects assault me at once.

"Here you are again. A man with a choice. Hand Gregory over to authorities and take a gamble with the justice system that he'll be punished. Or take justice into your own hands to administer that punishment yourself."

"No." I shake my head, trying to clear the very thought. But it's consuming.

"You could punish the driver who took the life of your precious Melanie, like you've longed to do. Reap your vengeance on a selfish man who was never punished for the life he stole."

My heart beats wildly. I fasten my eyes closed, breathing through the onslaught of raw pain and wrath.

"What will you choose?" Smith asks, an excited edge creeping into his voice. "I'm curious to see, Dr. West. I've been very impressed by you. So impressed, I feel we're akin."

"We're nothing alike. I promise you that."

His eyebrows raise. "What you choose not to see, isn't the same as denial. You're no longer blind." He steps toward the door.

Rage fires through me, and I finally move, making the effort toward Smith. "You're not going anywhere."

"Yes, I am. You're letting me walk out." He extends his hand, Gregory's location a barrier between us. "This one is a simple choice for you. A simple trade."

"Fuck." I grip my hair, turn to face the bar, and in the end, my weakness wins out.

I remove the Five of Cups from my jacket and slap it on the table. With a flip of my fingers, I send the card across the tabletop. He picks it up and analyzes it for a beat before he removes the deck from his pocket and slips the card on top.

"Until next time, Dr. West." He lays the envelope on the table, then leaves.

I let the true Arcana Killer walk out of my door.

I sit down at the table, in the same chair where he sat, and stare at the envelope. I hold it for what feels like hours before I finally work up the courage to tear it open.

The address of Gregory Miller puts him ten minutes away.

"Dammit."

There is no secret killer lair where Smith is keeping him.

He lied, and he could be lying about everything... But that grief latches on to the truth in his words. He bluffed me to get on the jury, and he bluffed me just now—but I'm still damn good at what I do.

I discerned the truth in his words about Gregory Miller.

And the pieces fit.

Melanie's killer has lived here all this time, passing our loft on his way home. Did he think of her as he drove by? Did he take a different route, avoiding the reminder?

Did he look up her name?

Did he visit her grave?

The questions plague me, and I will never have them.

Unless I get them.

I push the paper into my pocket and grab my phone. I make the call as I'm walking out, adrenaline rocketing through my system.

"Eddie. I know it's late, but listen closely and don't interrupt. I'm texting you the address of Porter's abductor. He's there now...and I need police at this location in less than ten minutes. Do it now."

I end the call.

Sometimes, fate is like flipping a coin. Heads you win. Tails you lose.

And then occasionally, there are no winners. Fate is a cruel, conniving bitch. We think we can best her, but it's always a toss up. A silver coin flipped in the mother fucking air.

What will you do?

In the video, when Porter was pleading to me...she begged me to do the right thing.

That question ricochets around my skull as I walk steadily, assuredly, toward the home of Melanie's killer. I pray—to fate, to Mel, to Porter—that the authorities get there first.

In a twisted world where pain is met around every corner, where it shrouds good with evil and mangles your insides, it's the only *right* thing I know to do.

EPILOGUE

FROM THE ARCANA KILLER

What do you see when you tear the veil away and stare into the closet? How many skeletons await you in that dark alcove?

What do your bones whisper to you at night, when the veil is the thinnest, when your demons claw from the inside? Every torturous pain you've inflicted, another slash of the razor-sharp talon. Your shame a blood-spattered canvas, torn and smeared with black earth.

Your truth cannot stay buried.

There's a devil with a Tarot deck waiting to challenge your fate.

Everyone has a card, a judgment day, just as everyone has a past. They go hand in hand. A tangled, patchwork quilt of suffering and guilt.

The truly treacherous souls feel nothing at all. They've numbed their pain. Some use drugs. Others sex, or money. Poison to leech the infection. But it's still there—that dark, vile secret, a devouring cancer.

I am not above you—we are the same. Our blood lets red

as it pools atop our coversheet. For the devil is a collection of bones and blood, a putrid amassing of all sins. My well is full. The decay has infected my very soul. I'm told, an inoperable aortic aneurysm—a ticking time bomb—is my fate.

I flip Death over, run my finger along the edge of the card.

Even the devil bows to fate.

In doing this for as long as I have, I've learned there are two types of people: Those who fear death, and those who welcome it. If you're curious which type you are, here's a test.

Imagine you're given a choice: you can die an excruciatingly painful death, or die a quick, painless death. Now imagine there's a catch. Die now and suffer no pain. Or die five days from now, and bear the agony of a truly horrid death.

Most people, believing they are brave, or wise, think they will opt for the pain-free demise. But when faced with the choice in the very moment of death, they deny the gift. They fight, and war, and rage against the end…just for a chance at a few more days.

It's the human condition. We are unable to accept the end —the *true* end. We want one more day, hour, minute. We will endure the agony for simply the promise of more time.

Is your heart racing? Breaths coming too fast?

Then your decision is made.

For Dr. Ian West, where he once welcomed an easy death, he is now a fighter.

Tasked with an impossible choice, he chose life—and he chose to gift that life to his enemy. He did so with the knowledge of the agonizing pain to come.

Did you make the connection? There was one within the message I had Shaver give to Dr. West. He didn't understand it then, but I wonder if he sees it now, if he's finally put all the parts together.

In order to accept this new vessel, he must follow the path that sets his adversary free, forsaking his principles.

In the end, Dr. West's true adversary was never Shaver; it was always the man without a face—until I gave him one. The bones of revenge haunting Dr. West's nightmares.

I admit, I might have judged him wrong. I watched, fascinated, as Dr. West sacrificed the kill and spared Gregory's life. I had thought I'd finally found the grief-burdened man in the cloak that would become my successor.

My salvation.

Before the time bomb in my body detonates, my soul has to be purged of all the sins I've consumed.

But…there is a small fraction of time left.

I shuffle my Tarot deck.

I lay the cards out until the Five of Cups appears. It always appears. I smile, wondering which unfortunate soul is struggling with their own five stages of grief.

I ask the cards: *who will be next?*

Five of Cups is just one of the many stories in the Cards of Love Collection. Which card will you choose next? Find the entire collection here: www.cardsofloveromance.com

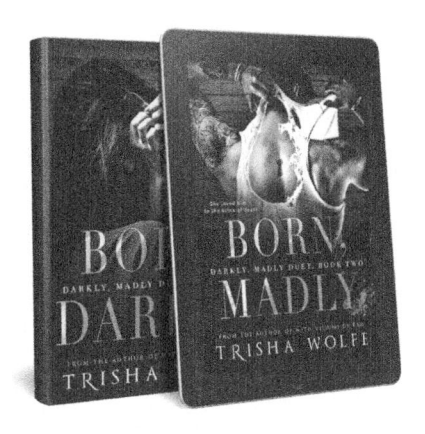

Start the Darkly, Madly Duet today. Criminal psychologist London Noble falls for her serial killer patient. Don't miss this psychologically thrilling romance.

www.TrishaWolfe.com

ALSO BY TRISHA WOLFE

Broken Bonds Series

With Visions of Red

With Ties that Bind

Derision

Darkly, Madly Duet

Born, Darkly

Born, Madly

Living Heartwood Novels

The Darkest Part

Losing Track

Fading Out

ACKNOWLEDGMENTS

Thank you to:

My amazingly talented critique partner and friend, P.T. Michelle, for reading so quickly, giving me much needed pep talks and advice, wonderful notes, and for your friendship.

My super human beta readers, who read on the fly and offer so much encouragement. I could not write books without your brilliance. Honestly, you are my girls! Melissa & Michell (My M&M's), and Debbie Higgins for reading quickly to give me helpful insight as always.

To the amazing gals in The Lair! I adore you so hard. You keep me sane, where it's perfectly acceptable to be anything but ;) Thank you for all that you do for me, my books. Thank you, girls.

To all the authors out there who share and give shouts outs. You know who you are, and you are amazing.

To my family. My son, Blue, who is my inspiration, thank you for being you. I love you. And my husband, Daniel (my turtle), for your support and owning your title as "the husband" at every book event. To my parents, Debbie and Al, for the emotional support, chocolate, and unconditional love.

Najla Qamber of Najla Qamber Designs, thank you so much for not just creating this stunning, take-my-breath-away cover, but for also rocking so hard! You are so much fun to worth with; you took the stress right out of the very stressful task of series cover creation, and I cannot wait to work with you again on future projects.

There are many, oh, so many people who I have to thank, who have been right beside me during this journey, and who will continue to be there, but I know I can't thank everyone here, the list would go on and on! So just know that I love you dearly. You know who you are, and I wouldn't be here without your support. Thank you so much.

To my readers, you have no idea how much I value and love each and every one of you. If it wasn't for you, none of this could be possible. As cliché as that sounds, I mean it from the bottom of my black heart; I adore you, and hope to always publish books that make you feel.

I owe everything to God, thank you for *everything*.

ABOUT THE AUTHOR

From an early age, Trisha Wolfe dreamed up imaginary worlds and characters and was accused of talking to herself. Today, she lives in South Carolina with her family and writes full time, using her imaginary worlds as an excuse to continue talking to herself. Get updates on future releases and special bonus material at www.TrishaWolfe.com

Made in the USA
Monee, IL
04 May 2023